Savage's Feud

When his Pinkerton supervisor handed Savage the job of finding a missing family somewhere in the south-west, neither expected it to lead to a vicious feud and a massacre. Nor did Savage expect to uncover a Southern outpost where the stars and bars of the Confederacy still flew proudly.

What had happened in the past to set the Howards and the Flints on their way to a bloodbath? And was there any truth in the story of a missing pay chest? These were just some of the baffling questions which Savage had to answer. In the meantime, he meets one woman who wants him dead and another who's seeking to hire a killer!

Only when there is a violent duel to the death will all the problems be resolved.

By the same author

Vermilion Springs' Vendetta
A Man Called Savage

Savage's Feud

SYDNEY J. BOUNDS

A Black Horse Western

ROBERT HALE · LONDON

© Sydney J. Bounds 2002
First published in Great Britain 2002

ISBN 0 7090 7099 3

Robert Hale Limited
Clerkenwell House
Clerkenwell Green
London EC1R 0HT

Typeset by
Derek Doyle & Associates, Liverpool.
Printed and bound in Great Britain by
Antony Rowe Limited, Wiltshire.

Contents

1

A Man Called Smith

Dave Bridger was sweating. He had his tie off and shirt-sleeves rolled up. The door and window of his small office over the bank were wide open, yet no breeze stirred the papers on his desk. The skin under his bushy whiskers itched, and he scratched. The air was so humid it felt like trying to breathe water.

He was used to New York heat but this was something more. The smell of Southern fried chicken drifting up from Fremont's Main Street reminded him of his home city's favourite boast; we fry eggs on our sidewalks!

Here, in the south-west, locals claimed that hens laid their eggs hard-boiled. Bridger hoped Mr Allan would recall him before he melted down to a grease-spot.

He was supposed to be holding the fort until a new territorial supervisor was appointed to replace Edsel, shot dead by bank robbers.

Originally, he'd been sent to get Edsel's killer, but young Savage had beaten him to that.

Bridger still wasn't sure how he felt about Savage, whether he'd fit into the Pinkerton organization. He was tough and a survivor, but maybe too much of a loner.

When Bridger had trapped him, a baby-faced kid with a carving knife, he'd named him Savage, and that was just what he was.* What else could you expect of a thief on New York's waterfront?

Mr Allan had decided to use one thief to destroy another, and Savage had done the job he was stuck with. No one else working alone, Bridger thought, could have smashed the two outlaw gangs terrorizing the south-west. Yet he still had some doubt; could the youngster be trusted? Bridger was sure he wouldn't care to present his back to him.

Savage was officially on sick leave, recovering fast from a gunshot wound; youth, he supposed. At his age, Bridger was sure he'd still be flat on his back, if not in a grave.

There was no doubt about it. The kid was adapting to this life, so the sooner a new supervisor was appointed the sooner he could get back where he belonged. The south-west was a frighteningly large territory to cover with a handful of agents, and Savage was the last one still in Fremont; and only till the doctor signed him off as fit.

Bridger knew where he was and guessed what

* See 'A Man called Savage'. Robert Hale, 2000

he was doing at this moment, and envied both his youth and stamina.

He heard footsteps on the wooden stairs and smiled. If this was a client, he'd get some satisfaction from interrupting Savage. The steps paused at the top of the stairs and Bridger called, 'Come in, take a seat.'

A tall man dressed in black entered, his face gaunt and unsmiling, his hair touched with grey. Easy to see him as an undertaker, Bridger thought, as his visitor settled into a chair across the desk, apparently unaffected by the heat.

Bridger envied his quiet calm as he felt a bead of sweat start down to his face, to evaporate before it reached his mouth. If the client carried a weapon it wasn't obvious, but there was muscle beneath the dark coat.

'My name is Smith –'

Maybe, Bridger thought, but for sure he was a Northerner, judging from his accent.

'—and I have a job for you. A missing family. Does your agency take that kind of job?'

'We take any kind that pays our rates.'

Smith nodded, as if he expected no less. 'I'll pay whatever you charge.'

Bridger opened a ledger and reached for a pencil to take notes.

'The name of the family is Howard, the head of the clan Joshua. Likely there are more of them by this time.'

Smith waited patiently while Bridger wrote this down.

'They came from the Deep South and moved
west after the war, which was when we lost touch.
The last I heard they were somewhere in the
south-west. When you find them, I'll have good
news ...'

Bridger raised his eyes to study the client, and
Smith gave a thin smile.

'Yes,' he repeated with emphasis: 'Good news!'

Savage stood naked before the window of a room
over the saloon opposite the Southwest and
Border Bank. Sweat ran down his wiry body, no
longer pale as the underside of a fish but beginning to assume the mahogany colour of a
Westerner. It was marked by an interesting scar;
at least, he reflected, women found it interesting.

The woman on the bed wore a pair of stockings
and looked old enough to be his mother. She
raised her head from a pillow and asked, 'Are yuh
coming back to bed?'

He watched her from the corner of his eye as he
stared from the window; outside the dust was
inches deep and the glare of sunlight strong
enough to dazzle. She represented no threat, but
he still trusted no one, man or woman.

Of course, he didn't truly remember his mother,
or father; they had died of influenza when he was
young. The authorities had intended to place him
in an institution, but he'd run and survived as a
loner ever since.

He had no further use for the woman; he'd
proved himself after his gunshot wound healed,

and now he was feeling restless.

Neither was he sure about the Pinkertons; the part he liked was the regular money, but he resented having to take orders and appear to stay with the law.

There was something about the south-west. He was beginning to acclimatize to the endless blue above an empty land; it spoke to a longing deep inside that he could never have imagined among the squalor of a city slum.

The woman rolled a cigarette and lit up. 'What's so interesting on Main?'

He stood watching a man enter the side entrance of the bank and start up the stairs leading to the Pinkerton Detective Agency. A man dressed in black with the calm assurance of an undertaker. A client?

Savage forgot the woman; he was all business now, fit and ready for action. He expected a summons from Bridger and began to dress. These days he wore Western clothes, except for flat-heeled boots.

She said sullenly, 'You lost interest all of a sudden. Just like a man – get what you want and then walk away.'

'Business,' he said, adjusting the Bowie knife clipped to his waist-belt. He tossed some dollar bills on the bed and went down the stairs and along the street.

At the Miner's Rest he collected his gear, moved down to a store to buy shells for his shotgun, then to a dry-goods store and finally to the livery.

11

'I need a horse,' he said. 'A quiet one that will last the distance. Charge it to Mr Bridger.'

The stableman selected a mare. 'This here's an Indian cayuse. Plenty of stamina, even if she ain't fully broken yet. If she gets frisky, let her run is my advice.'

Savage now had some riding experience behind him, and nodded. 'I'll be back,' he said leaving his saddle-bags with the mare. He walked along Main and climbed the stairs to the office.

'Saw him, did yuh?' Bridger grunted.

'Feller like an undertaker?'

'Yeah. He wants us to find a family named Howard, moved up from the south, then west, headman named Joshua. Last heard of in the south-west.'

'Big area.'

Bridger nodded. 'You're all right at street fighting – this is detective work. You need brain as well as brawn.'

He paused to lubricate his throat from a glass of water.

'The client agreed our terms and paid a deposit and you're the only agent available so you're it. Hunt out an old-timer with a memory who likes a drink and let him ramble. You get a lead and follow it to the next lead, wherever it takes you, and chase another lead. Eventually you'll stumble on a Howard. Nothing to it.'

'Nothing to it,' Savage echoed. 'Does this client have a name?'

'Calls himself Smith.' Bridger's lip curled. 'Out

of the thousands of genuine Smiths, I get a phoney. Watch yourself with this one. I never heard of anybody paying money to find someone to give them good news.'

'Doesn't sound reasonable,' Savage agreed.

He went slowly downstairs to Main and stood quietly in a patch of shade, watching the street. The sunlit side was deserted. A few women were shopping on the shady side. Idlers sat outside a saloon, drinking, smoking and gossiping. He scanned windows, wondering where Smith was now.

Why did he think it necessary to give an obviously false name? There was no sign of the man who looked like an undertaker, but Savage turned a corner and used back streets to reach Ringo's Place.

Ask around? The man who called himself Smith had probably done that already and got nowhere. Bridger might know how it was done in the big city, but out here folk tended to mind their own business and their mouths didn't flap. He decided that if Smith wasn't being straight with him, he might do better with those who were less than honest.

Ringo's was a hang-out for those with no visible means of support, men the law did not regard with favour. Men who would sell a Howard for a dollar – and a Smith for a few dollars more: drifters, petty thieves, human wrecks from the war.

Ringo had been a gunhawk till he lost the

fingers of his right hand to a Mexican wielding a machete; now he owned a back-street shop one step up from a slum, part saloon, part dining-room.

Savage entered quietly and sat in a corner where the light was dim. He ordered the cheapest meal and waited. When his meal came he ate slowly, concentrating on his food and avoiding the eyes of other customers.

Presently a scarecrow figure approached.

'Spare a quarter for a drink, mister?'

Savage looked up. Under the dirt and smell, the face was old and weathered. He took a small coin from his pocket, but kept his hand closed around it.

Hooded eyes watched his hand. Neither spoke; it was a delicate moment. Then feet shuffled. 'What d'yuh want to know?'

'Might have been a feller named Howard around here at one time.'

'Howard. Not a local name, that.' Lips licked in anticipation. 'Sure yuh got the name right?'

Savage waited in silence, apparently bored.

'Not around here. Maybe ...' A pause.

Savage took another coin from his pocket and added it to the first and kept a tight grip. 'Who might know?'

'Waal ... you a chancer, kid?'

'Don't call me "kid"!' For a moment, viciousness flared in Savage's eyes and his body tensed like a cat about to spring.

The old man stepped back in alarm. 'Yep, guess

you're a hard one. Guess you might find someone at the cantina to tell yuh what you want to know.' He pronounced the name as if there were only one such place.

Savage took another small coin from his pocket and added it to the two in his fist. 'Where's that? How do I get there?'

The old man mumbled something, and Savage leaned closer. 'Speak up.'

His informant shook his head, whispering.

'I ain't told yuh nothing, see ... ride the old Spanish trail to where it forks, then strike west. Must be sorta faded but I reckon you could still make it out. Further along there's what used to be a crossroads – and there's the cantina. Only folk needing to rest up out of sight use it.'

Savage nodded and opened his fist; the old man scooped up the coins and hurried to the bar.

Savage finished his meal and went outside. The worst of the day's heat was fading. He decided to start moving while the light lasted, collected his gear at the livery and saddled up. He asked the stableman to point him in the right direction for the old Spanish trail and rode out of town.

2
At the Cantina

Savage was not sorry when he saw the cantina sitting on the horizon. His muscles had stiffened during his enforced rest and the mare had tried some of her tricks on him; they'd only recently reached an understanding. He was hot and sweaty, with just a few precious drops of liquid at the bottom of his canteen.

He'd slept under the stars during darkness and various parts of his body disapproved of the hard-baked ground. The track west had been so faint from disuse he'd had to dismount more than once to be sure of it. He began to relax as the mare increased her pace.

Closer, the crossroads became almost obliterated and the cantina appeared more like a walled fort stuck in the middle of nowhere. The surrounding land was flat and featureless; no one was going to take anyone here by surprise.

The building was square with a tower at each corner, the outside walls blank. The single gate was open and Savage paused a moment; nailed to the solid wood was a human ear, an eyeball and a withered pair of lips. Trophies that suggested a Pinkerton agent would not be welcome.

He rode into the central plaza; rooms were built out from the walls.

In the middle of the plaza was a well and water-trough and he dismounted and pumped water for the mare. He cupped his hands and eased his throat, then filled his water-bottle in case he had to leave in a hurry.

Eyes watched him from beneath an awning. A dark-skinned boy approached.

'One dollar, *señor*, to take care of your horse.'

Savage paid him and noted where he stabled the mare, then beat the dust from his clothes. He walked to a table in the shade and sat easy. A fat man wearing a greasy apron came from inside.

'What I've got is goat with beans and peppers.'

'That'll be fine, with about a quart of coffee.'

He sat alone at a table, eating slowly, surrounded by armed men; unshaven and sunburnt, they were crammed together at tables out of the sun.

They talked idly among themselves, seeming to ignore him. Savage washed the peppers down with black coffee, listening without appearing to take more than casual notice. Their hands were never far from their guns as they smoked or drank, hard men used to a rough life outside the law.

One of them, with a bald head and a bottle of

whiskey was scowling and swearing.

'Those damned Howards! D'yuh hear they've put up the toll again?'

Another shrugged carelessly. 'It's pay, or risk someone catching up.'

A man with a scarred face interrupted: 'There's too many of them to tackle and they've got that valley sewn up. You want a quick route to get cattle up north, that's it. I don't see we've much choice.'

The bald-beaded man continued to drink and curse.

Savage pushed his plate aside and called for more coffee.

'You fellers talking about any particular Howard? One by the name of Joshua, maybe?'

Baldy glared at him. 'You friendly with Josh?'

'Just recently heard the name,' Savage said quietly.

'Josh is head of the clan,' Baldy said. 'The valley swarms with Howards and they stick like glue – they know damn well they've got the only safe way through the mountains, and they make sure nobody follows us.'

Savage considered this information. 'Guess there's a town north of this valley? And another way round to it?'

'Yeah, a town name of Rattle. You take the long way around and maybe somebody catches up and takes a look at your brand.'

Savage nodded. 'And the buyers in Rattle?'

'Another Howard there, running things. You

18

sound like a Northern man, so I advise yuh to steer clear.'

'Yeah?'

'That's good advice,' the scarred man said. 'The Howards are a real old-fashioned Southern family – mad about Dixie – and don't seem to recognize that the war's over.'

'I call that weird.'

'Sure is.'

Savage sat back, drinking coffee, reluctant to push his luck any further. 'Guess I'll—'

He heard a commotion outside the gate and all eyes turned towards two peons hustling a man into the plaza.

'A spy,' one called. 'Hiding behind the gate and listening.'

Savage tensed. The man seemed familiar, his dark coat covered in dust.

'You're making a mistake – I was simply dismounting to lead my horse inside.'

Baldy had a revolver in his hand, pointing, finger around the trigger.

'Bring him here! Reckon to perforate his eardrums so he won't listen in again.'

The man who could have been an undertaker saw Savage and appealed directly to him.

'Help me – you've heard of me as Smith. I can prove—'

Savage's face was like stone. He stood up, shotgun levelled and cocked.

'Maybe, and maybe not. You been following me?'

He was aware of revolvers sliding out of holsters,

some undoubtedly on a hair-trigger. This under-taker needed to contemplate his own funeral.

Smith waved a sheet of paper torn from a legal pad.

'Look at this – a receipt, see?'

Savage moved forward, bleak-faced, took the offered paper and palmed it. If the receipt had the Pinkerton name on it, he couldn't afford to let these men see it. Behind him he heard the sound of guns being cocked, and rammed the twin muzzles of his shotgun into Smith's stomach, forc-ing the air from his lungs before he could open his mouth again.

'I'll deal with this one,' he said coldly.

'Take him outside then,' Baldy said. 'You use a scatter-gun in here and you'll clean up the mess.'

'You heard. Outside.' Savage jabbed again with the shotgun and Smith turned and headed for the gate.

Savage felt an itch between his shoulder blades as he imagined the guns covering him. He whis-tled, and the mare came to him.

Beyond the gate, he said. 'Get on your horse and ride. Why the hell did yuh have to follow me? You damn near got us both killed.'

He swung into the saddle and turned away from the cantina.

'I can look after myself,' Smith said, and conjured a pistol from a shoulder holster under his coat.

'You want to go back to the cantina and try that trick? Alone?'

'All right, I was too keen – and I wasn't sure you were the right man for this job. But you've convinced me.'

He glanced sideways at Savage as they rode along and barked a laugh as funny as an open grave. 'You found the Howards and that's good news – for the Flints.'

'First Howards, now Flints.'

'My name's not Smith. I'm Homer Flint and now ...' He opened a fat wallet and pulled out a wad of banknotes. 'Consider this a down payment on a private job – there'll be more when you report back.'

Savage didn't count the notes; his hand closed about them and he stuffed them in his pocket. If Flint thought he'd see them again, he was wrong.

When Savage showed no further interest, Flint said, 'I want you to get into this valley. I want to know how many Howard men there are, where they have look-outs and the sort of weapons they have.'

Savage showed his teeth. 'You figuring on starting a war?'

'The Flints and the Howards have been feuding as long as anyone can remember; then suddenly they took off and we lost track of them.'

Homer looked round but nobody had left the cantina after them.

'We want to catch up and deal with them one last time. Either we wipe out the Howards or ...'

Savage grunted a monosyllable. He was no more convinced by this new story than the one

21

Homer had told Bridger; once a liar, always a liar. There was something odd going on and he was curious; besides, he liked the idea of taking money off Homer Flint.

'Waal,' he said finally, 'you've got me interested in the Howards and their valley – but you'll have to quit following me around like a stray dog. I'm used to working alone.'

'Then we must arrange a place to meet later.'

Savage thought about it. Any private deal needed to be away from Fremont and Bridger.

'Calico,' he said, remembering a small town from his past. 'There ain't many folk left there – must be near deserted by this time. You wait there till I come.'

'Calico,' Flint agreed. 'I'll be expecting yuh.'

They parted, and Savage headed his cayuse towards the mountains. This time he made sure he wasn't followed; he kept a sharp eye on his back trail till Flint became a distant speck, and vanished. Then he made a wide swing to get around the mountains.

He was aiming to come in from the north and look over the town of Rattle before he visited the Howards' valley. He rode into the foothills till he reached a river, dismounted and stripped to wash the dust from his body.

The mare moved upstream to drink and Savage murmured, 'I don't blame yuh, gal.'

The water was cold and clear as only a mountain stream can be. His teeth began to chatter when a sudden surge threatened to sweep him off his feet, bringing back an early memory.....

....of a time when he was green to the New York waterfront and ignorant of the casual cruelty of slum children. He was walking idly along a wharf when hands grabbed him, pulled him close to the edge and pushed him over.

His screech of 'I can't swim!' brought only mocking laughter. He'd seen a gang of kids chuck a dog in for fun, but he'd never imagined the day when it would be his turn.

Dark oily water closed over his head and he came up spluttering. He flailed his arms wildly as he gasped for air, swallowing a foul-tasting liquid. He felt desperate and knew he was going to drown as a current swept him away from the dockside.

He went under again amid jeers and laughter and realized there was no point in shouting for help; no one was going to come to his aid.

Panic threatened self-control, stripped him down to a need to survive. Panic wouldn't save him. He had to ... what? He remembered that the dogs didn't drown; they paddled to the shore, climbed out and shook the water out of their hair.

If a dog could do it, then he could. He moved his arms up and down, hands cupped and clawing at the water. He learnt to keep his mouth shut and his chin up to get his nostrils above the surface.

He kicked out with his legs and began to move through the filth and debris floating around him. He wasn't sinking, he wasn't drowning ... he was swimming, and now with a purpose.

He brushed water from his eyes so he could see the quayside. It looked a mile away but obviously could only be a few yards. He kept dog-paddling and, eventually, reached a rusting iron ladder coming down from the wharf.

He clutched at a rung and hung there, getting his breathing under control, spitting out rubbish with river water. He rested for several minutes, then hauled himself up the ladder. He sprawled on the quayside, soaking wet and stinking.

His mouth set in a hard line and his muscles bunched. He scrambled upright, hands clenched, and charged the boys who'd thrown him in.

They ran off, laughing and shouting: 'Beware, savage dog!'

3
One-Man Town

Savage drifted into Rattle from the north, knowing that any stranger would be the focus of waiting eyes, but hoping for no more than a casual
inspection. He held the mare to a walking pace,
his Stetson tilted forward to shield his face.

Coming down the wide dusty stretch of
Broadway, his gaze took in idlers on a bench,
saloons and stores, a marshal's office. Further
along he saw a two-storey hotel with a livery
stable next door and headed for it.

He'd thought his casual entry was going well
when, with no warning, the mare went stiff-
legged, nearly throwing him. She backed away,
shying and snorting. Savage cursed her for drawing attention to him before he saw the reason for
her behaviour.

Right in the middle of Broadway a rattlesnake
lay coiled, sunning itself. It was a big one, with
brown-and-ochre patterning, and its head lifted
and swayed, searching for what had disturbed it.

25

Savage had to concentrate on controlling the mare; she was being difficult, and he'd never sat a horse before coming West on his first job for Allan Pinkerton.

Gradually he edged her to one side, mounted the plankwalk and urged her towards the livery. A few idlers gave him a cheer.

A stablehand took the mare's reins as he slid from the saddle.

'Most folk use the back way in.'

'D'yuh mean you have snakes in town as a regular thing?'

The stableman shrugged. 'They were here first – it's how the town got its name. Some years there's a lot, others hardly any.' He led the mare back into cool shadow. 'She'll soon quieten down.'

'Give her corn,' Savage said. 'I'm taking a room at the hotel.' He picked up his shotgun and saddle-bags and walked next door. The desk clerk booked him a room upstairs, at the rear.

'Sorry, sir, the front's taken. We have cattle buyers in town.'

'I'm not too fussy,' Savage said, and went up carpeted stairs. The passage leading to his room had bare floorboards. He dropped his gear on the bed and looked from the windows at a back alley and a loading bay for a big store.

He went down to the dining-room and sat at a vacant table. A group of men appeared to have finished their meal and sat talking quietly over coffee and cigars; they were expensively dressed men who glanced towards him and then ignored him.

He ordered a meal and, while he waited, a townsman came in by the front entrance and stopped at his table.

'Danser, editor of the Rattle *Echo*. I like to meet visitors to see what news they've got for me. Somehow you don't look a cattle buyer, sir.'

Savage saw a middle-aged man in a shiny suit, slightly stooped, with steel-rimmed spectacles perched on a pointed nose. He carried a notepad and pencil.

'Perhaps you have other business in town, Mr ...? My readers are always interested in what visitors think of our town.'

'Name's Savage, and I figured I was forgetting what it's like to sleep in a real bed. Your town was on my horizon so here I am.'

'Come far, Mr Savage?'

'Far enough, Mr Danser. Do you own this paper?'

Danser looked uncomfortable. 'No, sir. Mr Christian Howard owns the *Echo*, and appointed me as editor. Mr Christian also owns other properties in Rattle if you're thinking of starting a business.'

Savage nodded. 'Message understood. If I decide to start something here, I'll be sure to let Mr Howard know first.'

After Danser left, Savage's meal came from the kitchen and he enjoyed a steak with hash browns and onions; so far, the food was the most impressive thing about Rattle.

It was obvious that Danser was checking up for his boss, which was interesting. He was in no hurry and asked for more coffee.

Another man entered the dining-room, looked around and walked straight towards him. This one wore a star and was armed.

'Archer, town marshal. Danser mentioned he didn't like the answers you gave.'

Savage stared at him, wondering. He saw a brocaded vest, twin pearl-handled revolvers and long hair that swept in a wave over broad shoulders.

'Guess you must be Howard's man too.'

Archer nodded. 'Mr Christian appointed me. Now, sir, what's your business here?'

'I'm not sure yet,' Savage admitted. 'I've just arrived and haven't had time to look around. Maybe I'll stay a few days.'

Archer said, 'We don't support drifters, Mr Savage, and Mr Christian owns this hotel.'

'So?'

'You may be asked to leave. He also owns the bank, the biggest store, the biggest saloon and more.'

Savage's smile was frosty. 'You mean, behave or leave town.'

'How you leave is up to you.'

'I'll keep that in mind, Mr Archer – and I'll leave when I'm ready.'

The marshal nodded curtly, turned and walked out of the dining-room.

*

Tom Archer left the hotel and crossed the street to a shop with a red-and-white striped pole above the door. Lew wasn't busy and Archer dropped into the chair in front of a mirror that faced the open door; that way he could keep an eye on Broadway.

Lew hovered, waving his scissors. 'The usual, Marshal?'

'The usual,' Archer confirmed. His long wavy hair didn't need much attention, but he found it restful to sit in Lew's comfortable chair; and useful to listen to his gossip.

'Seen the stranger?'

'Not yet. Heard of him though.' Lew used his scissors to snip a few stray ends and combed out a tangled wave.

Archer knew he didn't have to say more. Lew would keep his ears open and relay anything that came his way about the stranger.

He closed his eyes and relaxed. Savage ... a name that suited him. He'd met the type before; young and wild. But Savage wore no gunbelt and that was odd. Mostly they wanted to be gunfighters and that made him wonder about this one.

Archer was a generation older in experience; he'd made a name as one of the fastest on the draw. He opened his eyes to study the lined face in the mirror – and knew he wasn't as fast today, and that his sight wasn't what it had been at the height of his career.

A career as army scout, buffalo hunter and

hardcase; along with Wild Bill he'd hired out as town-tamer a time or two. Usually he could rely on his reputation to avoid a challenge; sometimes he called on his deputy to handle trouble. Yet there was something about young Savage that bothered him.

Of course, he could quit any time. He'd had offers, but Rattle suited him well enough; it was a quiet town, Mr Christian paid regularly and few men were going to challenge his grip on the town.

He didn't really want to leave; taming yet another cattle town was something best left to younger men. He'd just have to be careful till Savage left Rattle; after all, there was nothing to keep him here. So why had he come?

Savage had no real reason to stay. He knew now how rustlers could bring in stolen cattle and sell them without interference; but curiosity was strong.

He decided that, before investigating the valley, he would look over the town that Howard owned. He picked up his shotgun and stood in the hotel porch, looking both ways.

There were still people on the street, and subdued music came from a nearby saloon. Diagonally across the street was a solid stone building of a single storey; it was large and the sign read: HOWARD'S BANK; the door was open.

'Is there anything the man doesn't own?' he wondered aloud.

A small voice beside him murmured, 'Chinese

laundry.' Savage half-turned to see a smiling yellow face and a short pigtail.

'Wing Fat, sir. Wash and press best shirt, twenty-five cents. Look plenty smart for Saturday night dance with pretty lady.'

'Glad to hear there's some free enterprise in this town. If I'm here for the weekend, I'll do that.'

The sun was almost touching the roofs as it sank. 'Mr Howard works late.'

'Works almost as many hours as Chinese. Mr Christian hates to turn away a dollar.'

A bony figure came hurtling from the bank's doorway and landed in the dust of Broadway.

A large man followed him outside. His body, broad and thick as a gorilla's, was set on the top of bowed legs as if they could barely take the weight. He wore a check shirt, the sleeves rolled up to show dark hair that rippled as he flexed bulging muscles.

'Mr Milton,' Wing Fat murmured. 'Mr Christian's personal bodyguard.'

Milton picked up the scrawny man and pinned him against a wall with one hand and battered his face with the other. He wore iron rings made from horseshoe nails on his fingers, and the protruding heads of the nails ripped flesh and set blood flowing. A cheekbone cracked and the pain made the man moan.

'A homesteader wishing to borrow money,' Wing Fat murmured, and vanished as silently as he'd appeared.

'When Mr Christian says no ...' Milton empha-

31

sized each word with a blow, '...he means no. Now d'yuh understand?'

The homesteader mumbled through broken teeth. 'But my family—'

Milton smashed his nose with a final punch and dropped him.

Savage noticed that the marshal was watching the beating without interfering. Archer waited until Milton walked into the bank before moving.

He lifted the barely conscious man into the saddle of a mule, turned it loose and slapped it on the rump. The animal ambled slowly up Broadway on its way out of town.

It did not get that far. Once Archer's back was turned, someone led the mule to a hitching rail and lifted the homesteader on to the boardwalk. They vanished into a small house set back from the street.

Curious, Savage strolled in that direction. A neatly painted sign read: JACK WARD M.D.

It began to look as if Christian Howard didn't always get it all his own way; though Savage thought that if he needed to talk to the town boss, it would be better if Milton wasn't around.

For the moment, there didn't seem to be much future in further exploring Howard's town; he entered the nearest store and bought cans of tomatoes, hard biscuits and jerky. He checked that his mare was properly cared for and returned to the hotel, determined to leave early in the morning.

4
'A Dollar a Head!'

The sky beyond the window was beginning to lighten when he opened his eyes. He listened to sounds of activity for a few seconds, then scrambled out of bed to look. In the alley behind the hotel men were loading a wagon hitched to a team of horses; he saw boxes, crates and barrels carried from the store.

Savage dressed quickly and went down to breakfast, paid his bill and collected the mare. The marshal stood in the doorway of his office and watched him ride up the street and out of town. He saw no rattler this morning.

A mile or so out he left the track and sheltered among a group of cottonwoods. He dismounted and let the mare graze while he waited. Presently he heard the creaking of wagon wheels; the wagon was heavily laden and pulled by four horses.

A young man with a rifle sat up front with the driver; a metal badge glinted in the sun. The marshal's deputy was riding guard duty and looking too relaxed to be expecting trouble.

Savage smiled. If he'd figured it right, Mr Christian was supplying the valley Howards, so it didn't cost him anything extra to send the deputy along as guard. The wagon should lead him straight to the entrance.

He waited till it passed and got almost out of sight, then mounted and followed at a discreet distance. The land to one side rose steadily, forming a rock face as the trail dipped, and he left the wheel ruts to keep in the shadow of the cliff face, gradually catching up on the wagon.

He now had the advantage of shade and brush to cover his approach, and he let the mare slow to a walk as the sun rose higher and the temperature with it.

The wagon was only lumbering along when, suddenly, it vanished into a narrow opening in the face of the cliff. Inside the gap, the ground fell away.

Savage swung from the saddle and let the mare graze while he climbed the rock face; and the higher he climbed, the further into the valley he could see.

There was a right-angled turn just beyond the opening and this had been made into a checkpoint. Two armed men were in plain view. Rock walls rose in tiers on each side of the trail, and terraces of stone were lined with boulders an army could hide behind.

He almost laughed aloud at the idea of Flint trying to force an entry here. The wagon moved on and the entrance opened out into a broad and well-grassed valley. He was about to descend from his vantage point when he heard a clash of echoing hoofs.

He saw a cloud of dust rise and come closer; he crouched low to wait and watch. A herd of long-horned steers came charging in narrow file through the exit, urged on by dust-covered riders. Savage had little doubt these were stolen cattle and that the men driving them to market were thieves.

As the stream of cattle ended, riders bunched them and headed for Rattle and the waiting buyers. He had seen enough and climbed down.

He found his mare and began a wide loop to get around the mountains. As he rode south he considered Homer Flint and why he should be so keen to penetrate the valley.

He wondered, too, what the Howards would have to say about Flint if he ever got the chance to ask them. And what Dave Bridger's attitude would be to this new twist in the job he'd taken on.

For the moment, only one thing concerned him. There had to be an easier way into the valley.

'Frenchy' Lamont twisted in the saddle and fired his long-barrelled Colt at his pursuers. It didn't scare them off. His face a mask of sweat and dust, he concentrated again on driving the small herd before him.

'*Mon Dieu!* Damned greasers ...'

It was almost beyond belief that Mexicans

would chase him across the border and stay on his heels like this. They never had before.

That was why he'd cut his crew to a minimum, with a bigger profit for each when they sold the herd up north. This time he had only a couple of riders and Clem had already been wounded. Their situation did not look healthy.

Lead was flying recklessly as the Mexicans came on, determined to get back their cattle. Their cattle! That was a joke. These longhorns ran wild and were anybody's for the taking – at least, that was how Frenchy looked at it.

He kept his head down and used spurs to get a bit more speed from his mount. The cattle were running, no problem there. Dust choked his throat and he pulled down his bandanna to spit. A bullet removed his hat and his long reddish-brown hair streamed out.

'*Sacré* Mary, protect me!'

If he could reach the mouth of the valley he was safe, but that was still a distance away and the Mexicans were getting closer all the time. Bullets buzzed like hornets around his ears. If a stray slug caught his horse, he was in trouble. He felt disgusted ... running before a bunch of greasers!

But his pursuers had the numbers; they were excited, bawling threats and shouting as they pushed their horses hard. Frenchy cursed his luck.

Savage was in no hurry; he had food in his belly, money in his pocket and the mare was carrying him south towards the other end of the Howards'

36

valley. The heat of the sun forced him to move leisurely in whatever shade he could find, resting when it suited him and tasting fresh water at each small stream.

Eventually the mountains fell behind him and a sea of short brown grass stretched away for ever.

'Time for work, Horse,' he murmured, and turned her head in the direction he knew the valley must lie. Dust hung like a veil and the air trembled. Cattle were running his way, at speed.

Stampede! he thought, and urged the mare aside to let the herd pass.

Then, above the thunder of hoofs he heard a crackle of gunfire. If this were a rustling outfit making north for the valley they were being chased.

A horseman passed him, clinging to the saddle horn, his shirt stained red. The pursuers showed: Mexicans! Savage smiled. This could be his ticket to get inside, and he nudged the mare's flanks with his heels.

She went forward with a rush and he brought up his shotgun. The last of the steers passed, and he drew alongside the leading Mexican.

The man had a big moustache and scowled at him, and Savage let him have the first barrel. The Mexican slumped sideways and his horse carried him away.

Bullets flew past him and Savage ignored them; few men could shoot accurately from the saddle of a galloping horse.

He closed with another Mexican and triggered the second barrel, reloading as he rose to join up with the rustlers.

A slim man with reddish hair showed white teeth in a smile.

'Welcome, *mon ami*. I think you have scared them away!'

Savage slackened pace and looked around. He saw that the Mexicans had turned back.

'They've got some nerve invading our country like that,' he said. 'They're supposed to stay their side of the Rio.'

'*Oui, m'sieur* – while we ride anywhere!' The rustler winked. 'Lamont is my name, but everyone calls me Frenchy.'

'Savage.'

Gradually the running cattle slowed and Frenchy moved close to the injured rustler.

'How bad is it, Clem?'

'Lump of lead tore a chunk out of my right arm.'

Clem looked pale from loss of blood, and they stopped long enough for Frenchy to wash the wound, put a pad over it and bind it up.

'You'll live till we get to Doctor Jack in town.'

Frenchy's other rider joined them. 'The herd's slowing – and running the way we want.'

'Our luck has changed since M'sieur Savage joined us, Pete.' Frenchy turned to Savage. 'As you see, I'm short-handed for this job. If you stick with us to the delivery point, I'll cut you in for a share.'

Savage shrugged. 'Why not? I've nothing else on hand.'

Pete wasn't enthusiastic. 'Hell, we took all the risk, cutting out these cattle ...'

Frenchy gave him a hard look. 'You are forgetting, Pete, that without our new *ami* we would likely see no profit at all.'

Clem nodded. 'He's right, Pete.'

They rode after the cattle, herding them together as the land narrowed to a funnel between high rocks.

'I suggest,' Frenchy said, 'that you don't say much when we get inside – these Howards have a dislike for men from the north. And your accent will give you away every time.'

'Heard something of them,' Savage admitted. 'What are they really like?'

'Greedy! Each time we come this way, the only safe way – *mon Dieu!* – the toll charge goes up.'

The ground rose on each side as the opening into the valley became narrower. Savage kept his bandanna over his mouth and nostrils to avoid eating dust.

Now the land changed to bare rock as the animals slowed and, finally, halted. He saw a wrought-iron gate barring their passage; this was opened to permit one steer at a time to pass through. A half-dozen men, all heavily armed, supervised the operation, while a tall man counted in tens and then crossed through his marks. High above the check-out an armed look-out perched in shadow on the rock wall.

One of the Howards called out, 'It's a dollar a head this trip, Frenchy.'

'And one steer for the pot,' another added.

'Jeez,' Pete muttered, looking towards Savage. 'Our cut gets smaller all the time. Soon it won't be worth while bringing cattle north.'

'Heard some shooting back there.'

Clem indicated his bandaged arm. 'Damned greasers followed us.'

'Mexicans? This side of the border?' The speaker sounded incredulous.

Another Howard laughed, then jerked a thumb at Savage. 'Who's this, Frenchy?'

'M'sieur Savage. He came to our aid when the Mexicans attacked.'

Savage lowered his bandanna and spoke in a slow drawl. It wouldn't pass as Southern speech, but he hoped his northern origin wouldn't be so obvious.

'Just happened by at the right time.'

The questioner looked closely at him, and nodded. Apparently he'd passed, and he rode into the valley alongside the cattle. Once inside he relaxed.

Further down the valley, where it broadened out, the herd slowed to drink from a pool; the level of water remained the same and Savage assumed it was fed by an underground stream. A long wooden hut bore the sign: *Eats Here*.

'For us,' Frenchy said. 'We're kept separate from the family.'

There were small houses scattered all about, corrals and a barn. Behind them, on a slight rise, stood one large house with a veranda; in front of this was a flagpole. Savage looked at the flag and wondered what he was seeing.

'The Stars and Bars,' Frenchy said quietly, 'the flag of the Confederate States of America. If you're asked to salute it, don't hesitate. Joshua Howard takes this seriously.'

Savage nodded. It had been years since the war ended and the South admitted defeat; anyone who could still believe in the Confederate cause must be addled.

'I never figure on arguing with a loony.'

'Watch your tongue, *mon ami*, here he comes.'

Savage glanced around and saw a tall man, broad across the chest, maybe sixty, with a black bush for a beard. He was reminded of biblical pictures of an old-time patriarch.

Joshua Howard came striding across open ground towards them, an impressive figure in a long coat and dark sombrero. He appeared to be unarmed; Savage figured the rest of the Howards carried so many guns between them that this one didn't need to.

'I have been told,' his voice boomed out like a preacher reading the sermon in a large and empty church, 'that Mexicans attacked you. Are you sure, Frenchy, that they were truly Mexicans and not that spawn of Satan, the Flints?'

'I'm sure, Joshua.'

The patriarch's gaze roamed over the four of them.

'Clem is wounded, and you have a new man.'

'Calls himself Savage – he arrived in time to help us.'

41

Joshua stared at him. 'You are welcome, Mr Savage.'

Under the piercing gaze, Savage knew he daren't even try to fake a Southern drawl. He kept silent.

'You have nothing to fear here, providing you are not a Flint – a pox on that tribe! Any man outside the law of the United States is welcome. Explain to me how you came to be near enough to aid Frenchy.'

'I had some trouble with the law back East and made it as far as the cantina. Feller there told me nobody followed any outfit coming through this valley.'

'That is so, Mr Savage. What knowledge have you of the Flints?'

'Heard the name, is all.'

Joshua nodded, breathing heavily, his face dark.

'You will do well to avoid the breed. An idle lot, and the devil finds work for idle hands, as we know to our cost. Any Flint we unmask must be sent to his master in hell by special delivery. They lie, they cheat and they rob.'

Savage nodded respectfully. Homer Flint was a liar, that was certain.

His gaze moved past Joshua to a young woman coming down wooden steps from the veranda of the big house. She wore a fancy gown, cut low about the shoulders to give an enticing view of her figure. She was smoking strong tobacco in a pipe; but not even that could

42

hide the scent that preceded her.

The patriarch turned his head, smirking. 'My daughter, Naomi. As you may discover, Mr Savage, she has a romantic nature.'

Naomi moved with the ease of a trained dancer, her smile an open invitation. Her gaze was fixed on him; a man-eater for sure, and he was the new man in the valley.

She ignored her father, who walked away.

'I don't suppose,' she drawled, 'that you have any tobacco to spare?'

'Sorry, ma'am,' Savage said, removing his hat. 'I don't smoke.'

Pete was quick to offer her the makings, but she ignored him. His face flushed scarlet and he glowered at Savage.

'I don't suppose you drink either?'

'That's right, ma'am.'

'Or visit a loving woman?' Her eyebrows arched.

Savage smiled. 'It would be a pleasure to visit you any time, ma'am.'

A snap came into her voice. 'My room in the big house, nine o'clock tonight.' She turned and walked off.

Clem laughed. 'Sure's a lot of woman, that one.'

Frenchy nodded. 'And a dangerous one, too. Take care, *mon ami.*'

Pete said, 'If she scares yuh, I'll go in your place.'

Savage ignored him; he wasn't going to refuse her offer. He had yet to meet the woman he could-

43

n't subdue, and he hoped to persuade her to reveal something more than herself – with luck, something about the Flint/Howard feud.

After he'd eaten, he washed in the cattle pond and borrowed a razor.

Pete jeered. 'Jeez, that's only baby fuzz yuh got there!'

Savage reacted fast, pinning Pete to the wall of the dining-shack with the open razor touching his throat.

Frenchy pulled him back. 'No! I've still got cattle to move, *m'sieur.*'

Savage calmed and released Pete. He banged the dust from his clothes and set off for the big house in silence.

5
The Devil's Hole

He walked up rising ground to where the house sat on the crest. Lights in the windows were like eyes watching him. The sky darkened and horses in the corral turned their heads to stare as he passed by. No doubt there were men behind watching too.

He felt like top billing in a show as he went up steps to the veranda. The main door swung open to reveal an ebony-dark face.

'Mr Savage, sir, I'm Naomi's maid. I'll take your hat and – no guns? Your knife then.'

He handed her his Stetson. 'I'll keep the knife – Naomi may want some fruit peeled.'

'Follow me, sir.'

The house was quiet and the two of them made only a whisper of sound going up carpeted stairs. There was silence and shadow everywhere. If other people were nearby, they must be holding their breath, he thought.

At the top of the stairs was a short passage and a closed door at the end. The maid tapped lightly and opened it.

'Mr Savage,' she announced softly.

The bedroom was shadowed, with thick curtains across the windows and he paused, getting his bearings.

He saw an oil-lamp, turned low, and a bed, wide, deep and inviting. Yellow light spilled over Naomi as she changed position on the bed; she wore a flimsy shift and the light reflected off different planes of her body as she moved. She began to remove the shift, slowly, seductively.

Savage, excited, undressed quickly, dropping his clothes on the floor and placing his knife on top. She started to rise to meet him, lips parted, but he roughly pushed her back and sprawled over her. He sensed her urgency as they grappled flesh to flesh; she wrapped her legs around him and moved in time with him.

After he'd exhausted himself he could have collapsed but she urged, 'Again ... again.' She was an enthusiast and he did his best to fuel her lust, but it had been a long day. His intention to ask questions disguised as pillow-talk faded; his eyes refused to stay open and he slid into a satisfied and sweaty sleep.

He was not sure what woke him. He became suddenly aware that he was alone in the bed, and groped for his knife. It wasn't to hand and he came alert.

Savage's Feud

Naomi stood beside the bed, going through the pockets of his clothes.

'You bitch!'

He lunged for her, but she had his big Bowie knife and lashed out wildly. He swerved aside, missing his grasp.

She opened her mouth in an animal scream and backed away. The door slammed open and armed men rushed in. Savage turned to face them, naked and weaponless, teeth bared in a snarl.

Naomi waved a piece of paper. 'A spy!'

Desperately, Savage tried again to get the knife from her. A foot tripped him and his head struck a hard wooden door. Dazed, he turned, at bay, his back against a wall.

A gang of Howards crowded him into a corner, flailing at him with guns and clubs. Savage used his teeth and nails, drawing blood and tearing flesh. He gouged at a man's eyes, and someone swore.

'Regular little savage, ain't he?'

What saved him was the smallness of the room and the large knot of men trying to get at him; they got in each other's way. But he was hopelessly outnumbered and beaten to his knees. Still he fought back until a boot crashed into the lower part of his spine and he collapsed in agony.

Heavy boots smashed into him and he curled into a ball.

Naomi shrieked, 'Kill him, Michael. He raped me. Kill him!'

Michael was big and angry and tried his hardest to obey.

47

'Rape my wife, will yuh!' He hit Savage with a nail-studded club and kicked him as he tried to crawl away.

A powerful voice boomed, 'Enough, Michael, I wish to question this man. Make yourself decent, woman.'

Savage felt himself dragged upright, his muscles screaming with pain. His head slumped on his chest and blood greased his body so the hands holding him slipped and he fell.

Joshua Howard frowned. 'Naomi, what is it you have there?'

She handed her father the sheet of paper she'd taken from Savage's pocket; casually she slipped on her shift in front of admiring eyes.

Joshua turned up the oil lamp and read carefully.

'A receipt from the office of the Pinkerton Detective Agency in Fremont – made out to Mr Smith.'

Should have destroyed that, Savage thought dully; too late now. Two men held him upright.

'Who is Mr Smith?'

Savage spat out blood and Joshua stepped back a pace.

Someone prodded him in the small of the back with a gun-barrel.

'Speak up, spy, or I'll put a bullet in your spine.'

Savage concentrated on taking air into his lungs, and Joshua waited patiently.

'He told us his name was Smith; later he claimed to be Homer Flint.'

'That devil's spawn!' Joshua flared up at once. 'And you helped him.'

'I was blackmailed into it,' Savage said. 'Allan Pinkerton's got something on me.'

'Anyone who helps a Flint, in any way at all, is our sworn enemy.'

'Waal, maybe I can help you. Maybe I can deliver this Homer Flint straight into your hands.'

Joshua's face became like stone. 'And maybe you'd like us to turn you loose so you can lead a pack of Flints here.' He shook his head. 'No, Mr Savage, I can't trust you.'

Joshua took a deep breath. 'We will not suffer a Flint to live – or anybody who helps one. This,' he held aloft the receipt, 'is your death warrant, and when I lay hands on Homer I shall strip the flesh from his bones as lovingly as a father chastises a favourite son.'

Michael Howard licked his lips in anticipation. 'We can start with this one. Let me – I'd like that.'

Joshua looked Savage over with some care. 'No, I don't think so, Michael.'

'But—'

'This is no cringing Flint to whimper under the lash. He might collapse, he might die on us, but I can't see him howling for mercy the way I want to hear Homer howl. Lock him away until our guests have departed for Rattle.'

He turned to Naomi. 'Daughter, you will inform Frenchy and his men in the morning that Mr Savage cannot bear to leave your loving arms just yet – that he will rejoin them later.'

Another Howard asked, 'The cells, is it, Josh?'

Joshua nodded sombrely. 'Yes, the cellar – and then the Devil's Hole.' He made a warm smile for Savage. 'You shall have time to make your peace before you come to Judgement.

Two Howards half-marched, half-carried, him downstairs, then further down uncarpeted steps. There was a solid door fitted with bolts on the outside; he was thrust into darkness. The door slammed behind him and he heard iron bolts rammed home.

He felt a rough wall, more steps going down, and fumbled his way to the bottom. He sat on the last step leaning his head and shoulders against a wall. His mouth was dry and he wondered if they kept anything liquid in the cellar. He forced himself upright and felt his way around the walls, his bruised and aching body hurting.

He moved slowly, exploring by touch. The cellar was not large, the walls bare, part stone, part hard-packed earth. The room was empty – just a prison – except for a raised metal disc in the middle of the floor; he was too weak to lift it.

He stretched out on the floor and relaxed; he dozed, losing track of time. When he woke he felt hungry. He lurched upright, stiff and sore, and tried a few exercises to get his muscles working again. A cold chill had seeped into his body, numbing him.

He had no idea how much time had passed. At a guess, several hours. He emptied his bladder in a corner. Then he heard the bolt pulled back and light shone down as the door opened. He blinked.

Four men came down the steps, big heavy men with muscle. Savage faced them, hands clawed, calculating his chances; nothing he would be tempted to bet on.

Michael followed, a revolver in one hand and a lantern in the other. Then came Joshua Howard and Naomi, her eyes shining.

'Your friends have gone,' the patriarch said. 'So now it is your turn. What have you told Homer Flint?' He paused, waiting. 'It seems that, although you are a Yankee, you managed to discover our valley. How?'

Savage flexed his muscles, getting ready for whatever was coming.

'That wasn't difficult. rustlers make use of this valley, and word gets around.'

'I suppose so.' Joshua stood quietly, thinking. 'It seems then we must prepare to meet the Flints.' He sighed. 'Open the Devil's Hole.'

Two men got their fingers under slots in the metal disc, and heaved. The heavy cover clanged as they dropped it to one side. A circular hole showed in the floor; dark, with no indication how deep it might be.

'We call it by this name,' Joshua said, 'because no one has returned after the evil one has claimed a soul.'

He made a hand signal and the four bruisers closed in.

'Naked came ye into the world, and naked ye

leave it.'

Savage lashed out; his arm was trapped and held. A second man hit him in the stomach so he doubled over, the air forced from his lungs. A third rabbit-punched him, and the fourth kicked his legs from under him.

They've done this before, he thought dully as he was dragged to the edge.

'Careful,' Joshua warned. 'Do not damage him more than necessary – for the punishment to be fully effective he must be conscious as he falls. Anticipation is everything. Relax, Mr Savage, you will need such strength as you have left when you hit bottom.'

'I'll be back,' Savage shouted. 'I'll kill every damned Howard in this valley if I have to haunt you to death!'

Michael sneered. 'Want to bet?'

Savage was lifted off his feet and thrown at the gaping hole. As he fell into darkness he heard Naomi's mocking laughter.

Homer Flint sat on the veranda of the hotel in Calico, wearing his dark suit and brooding on how much longer he could afford to wait. The town had a dead feel to it. Savage had been smart to choose this place; anywhere else and there'd have been pointed questions about a gathering of armed men.

Maybe Savage was smart enough to get into the Howards' valley, and out in one piece.

He stared along a near-empty road to the fire-gutted area below West Street. The hotel man made out by renting rooms to anyone travelling through. A saloon kept going on the derelicts who had nowhere else to drink. The few survivors cared only about how much the Flints had to spend. A half-empty store did little business.

Of course, nothing was perfect. The older members of the clan respected him and followed his orders; it was the young ones who were impatient.

How much longer could he control those of an age to rebel naturally against authority? The hotheads who were reluctant to wait, who wanted action how.

Especially young Jason. Homer wanted to move against the Howards, but he understood the importance of knowing the enemy's strength. Intelligence first, then planning, finally action and a successful conclusion.

He watched three young Flints walk along the dusty street towards him, Jason in the lead.

Jason just wanted to kill Howards and take what was rightfully theirs. Homer agreed this was a proper attitude for a Flint and the reason the clan was gathering in this near-deserted backwater. But he also knew he was right to wait.

A faint smile creased his face as he wondered how Jason would try to pressure him this time. He composed himself to wait till the three young men reached him.

Jason was tall and willowy and considered himself a knife-fighter; he wore one now in a scabbard riveted to his waist-belt. He moved with confidence; over-confidence, Homer thought with a frown, and that made him a danger to the young who aped his ways.

Jason was tolerated by the older Flints, the war veterans who knew about the Howards at first hand. But what was it the young really believed?

Homer waited patiently, with the air of an undertaker measuring a young upstart for his coffin; he had, he reflected, buried a few in his time.

Jason stopped, facing him, and said, 'This man, Savage – he's an outsider. A Pinkerton man, you said.'

'A Northerner, like us. By his accent, I'd say New York. A genuine Yankee.'

'But not a Flint?'

'No.'

'So an outsider.'

'Yes.'

'We don't need an outsider. He must be eliminated.'

'Perhaps,' Homer said, 'but not yet. Not till he's brought the information I need.'

'But eliminated,' Jason insisted.

Homer said flatly, 'When the time comes, we'll vote on it. That is our way, as you well know.'

Jason smiled broadly. He knew how the vote would go because he'd impressed his views on the younger members of the clan – and they outnumbered the old ones.

'Good enough,' he said, and swaggered away, followed by his lieutenants.

6
No Way Back

Panic swamped Savage as he tried – desperately – for the edge of the hole, missed, and felt himself falling into darkness. He tried to straighten his body, to grab any projection to cling to, but only lost some skin and tore a fingernail. He scissored his legs and stuck for a moment, suspended head down till the blood rushed to his brain; then he slipped and continued his fall. The hole wasn't all that wide and he bumped from side to side.

Above him the circle of light went out and he heard the heavy iron disc drop into place in the cellar floor; it sounded like the beat of a drum signalling his doom. Even if he somehow survived the fall and climbed up, he knew he'd never be able to push up that weight of metal from below.

His shoulder struck something which stopped his descent with a jolt that rattled the teeth in his head. He could be sure of nothing in the blackness all around; had he hit a ledge? It seemed too soft.

It squelched as he moved and his fingers dug into something slimy that smelt unpleasant.

He was precariously balanced, teetering on an edge and he felt himself sliding. He groped with his fingers but found nothing solid to grip.

A strangely familiar sound came from below as he slid from his perch and fell again; running water. Must be an underground river, he thought: anything was better than rock to hit at the bottom when he …

… he struck water and went under. Icy cold from the mountains. It took his breath away and sucked the heat from his body. So he might drown, or freeze, but wouldn't die of thirst.

He broke surface, spluttering, panting for air. A current carried him along; the river was deep enough for him to swim and he dog-paddled, remembering to keep his chin high.

A strong swimmer might have gone against the current, but Savage wasn't that good. He was swept along, banging from side to side, the uneven rock taking off more skin. His feet couldn't touch bottom, but when he raised an arm, he struck the roof. It was lucky there hadn't been any rain for a while.

He was tiring and began to sink, groped for any projection to hang on to for a breather. Nothing. He kept dog-paddling along, cursing the Howards and swearing revenge. A strong hate was building and this kept him going.

He recalled his words: *I'll be back … I'll kill every damned Howard in this valley!*

Those weren't empty words any longer. He had survived and would claim his revenge. The feud had become personal.

The noise of the water changed and Savage wondered what was coming. There was not the faintest glimmer of light to see by. He heard a rushing sound of water over rocks that echoed and boomed in the confined space.

His feet briefly touched smooth rock and then he was carried over and down.

Joshua Howard had been walking in the valley he'd made his own; these days he favoured walking over riding when his mind was troubled. The sun was high when he got back, the Stars and Bars flag hanging limp in air almost too hot to breathe.

He removed his black sombrero and wiped the sweat-band as he paused beneath the veranda. He heard raised voices.

'You will—'

'I won't! I won't!'

Joshua frowned; his daughter and her husband were at it again. It was certain Naomi didn't take after her mother; Grace had disagreed more subtly and usually won her point. If she had lived, how differently things might have turned out.

Michael made a worthy husband, if slow in his thinking; slow but thorough. Give him a job to do and he would stay with it and see it done right.

At the moment, Joshua could do nothing to persuade Christian, who was not being as helpful as he might. But this other matter ...

He lifted his voice so it cracked like a whip.

'A God-fearing wife obeys her husband in all things. Go to your room, daughter, and pray for guidance. I wish to speak with Michael.'

His son-in-law came down the steps from the veranda, his face sullen.

'Yes, Josh, what is it now?'

Joshua spoke mildly. 'Try not to be so angry, Michael. It is not all Naomi's fault. I have asked more of her than I should, but that is ended. We can expect an attack by the Flint clan so there is no need to persuade visitors to talk. Homer hired a spy, so they're coming. Nothing is more certain.'

'But Naomi likes to—'

'Listen to me! What matters is that the spy so easily got into our valley. It should not have happened. If it hadn't been for your wife, he might have got out just as easily – with information of value to that brood of the devil.'

Michael said, resentfully, 'That don't make it right.'

'I agree, but I have a job for you. You will be responsible for tightening security at both entrances. Impress on the guards they must be more careful who they allow in. Make regular visits to each end of the valley and make sure they take their duties seriously. We cannot afford to be taken by surprise when the Flints strike.'

Michael looked pleased. It was the first time he'd been trusted with an important job. At last, it seemed, he was accepted.

He smiled cheerfully, forgetting the past. 'Yes, Josh, I'll start now.'

Joshua Howard watched him hurry towards the corral and saddle his horse.

Water sprayed into his eyes and mouth and got up his nose. A waterfall, Savage realized. He was standing in a shallow pool under the fall, lost his balance and submerged and was carried along, banging against rocks.

It was difficult to breathe and he struggled to get his head up. He clamped his mouth shut and started to paddle again.

The water was moving faster and there could be no way back; he'd never climb a waterfall. His arms and legs ached and he longed for a rest; he groped for a crag, anything to cling to for a few minutes.

A rock banged against his head, partially stunning him; a salty liquid trickled into his mouth. The roof was lower here, the passage narrower, the water level rising. If it continued he would be trapped in a water-filled tunnel with no air.

His fingers found cracks and he gripped as tight as he could, clinging there with his nose just above the surface, his legs swept almost horizontal by the current. He couldn't hold on for long. If only he could *see* ...

He'd have to let go eventually, pass through the tunnel and hope there was air again further on. He filled his lungs with short intakes; breathe in, hold it, breathe in, hold it, breathe in. When he

was sure his lungs could hold no more, he let go
and the current drew him along, forcing him
through....

Archer stood on the boardwalk outside his office
on Rattle's Broadway as a wagon rolled into town.
He was alert, watching men and horses and door-
ways as it pulled up outside the bank.

He didn't expect trouble; it was just part of his
job as town marshal to keep an eye on the wagon
as it returned from its regular run to the valley. It
would be carrying cash in exchange for the
supplies it had delivered.

No one local would attempt to rob Christian
Howard; his temper was too well known. He
owned property in town and land outside its
boundary, and his greed where a dollar was
concerned was a byword throughout the territory.
His bodyguard, Milton, was feared. And Archer
himself had a reputation as a gunfighter.

It would be a bold – and stupid – man who tried
to take a nickel off Christian Howard.

Eddie stayed on top of the wagon, rifle ready for
action. The driver climbed down, hefted a money-
bag, padlocked, and carried it into Howard's bank.

Archer moved along the plankwalk.

'Hi Eddie. Quiet trip?'

The deputy glanced down, relaxing. 'As always
– nothing ever happens.'

'Let's not get over-confident. Any news?'

Eddie rolled a cigarette and lit it.

'Josh reckons that he caught a snooper – a

61

Pinkerton man – hired by the Flints, of course.'

'Of course. Everything bad comes down to the Flints, according to Josh. Does this snooper have a name?'

'Called himself Savage.'

Archer tensed. 'Savage? There was an *hombre* using that name here, a while back. Snooping? Did Josh know anything else about him?'

'No, just said the Flints hired a Pinkerton man to find them.'

'If he really was ... I don't like the sound of this. Guess I'll mention it to Mr Christian.'

'Why bother?' Eddie said carelessly. 'He won't make no trouble. Josh chucked him down the Devil's Hole.'

The marshal frowned. 'Why didn't he buy him off? If somebody – never mind who – hired a detective agency to investigate the valley and he doesn't report ... waal, an outfit like the Pinkertons is likely to send another man to check on the first. And on Rattle as well. Keep me informed if Josh says anything more next time.'

He started towards the open doorway of the bank.

'I'll let Mr Christian know. You see Danser. Tell him to be extra sharp next time a stranger hits town. And keep your lip buttoned. Mr Christian won't want the cattle buyers getting cold feet.'

7

Brother to the Owl

Savage thought he was going to black out. His lungs felt as if they would burst any second as he was swept by a powerful current through a water-filled tube in solid rock. He held his nostrils pinched together with the fingers of one hand, his lips tight-pressed, his other hand raised up to touch the roof.

So far there was no trace of the air pocket he needed. That was scary because he was helpless and couldn't hold his breath much longer. He concentrated on the Howards and what he was going to do to them, blotting out everything beyond hatred and vengeance.

Rocks scraped his flesh and he was numb with cold, colder than he'd ever thought possible. Darkness was total.

He heard water gushing, so one ear was above the surface. He grasped a projection and hauled his nose and mouth up and let air out slowly. He gulped in fresh air. He was panting and he fought to control his breathing.

Blood trickled down his face and into his mouth. He spat it out. He was shaking, but daren't rest for long, just long enough to regain his calm; then he released his grip and the current swept him along once more. Head up, he resumed his dog-paddle.

He came to another tight place where he had to take in air and make it last, but he found this tunnel a closer fit. He stuck like a cork in a bottle-neck and had to struggle to free himself, fighting down panic and scraping yet more skin away. When finally he burst through, it was with a feeling of relief as his head surfaced and he drank in air again.

Further on the water-level dropped and he could stand. A stone in the shallows provided a seat and he rested, shivering. He knew he had to continue before he froze.

He was going to survive, he told himself; he was going to live and return to the valley and deal with those who had thrown him into the Devil's Hole.

He struggled on, going with the flow of water, dog-paddling as the level rose again, then wading as it fell. The river had to end sometime; it had to come out somewhere.

It was dark. He was wet and cold. And there came a point when he grew aware of the weight of rock above his head and imagined it pressing down, falling, crushing him. He had to fight off a feeling of walls closing in, squeezing him.

Something smelled differently, the air tasted fresher, but his strength was failing. He was shivering violently and had to concentrate, to force himself to go on.

He was reaching a state of collapse; his legs no longer seemed attached to his body and his arms flailed uselessly. He was close to the end when he imagined a pin-prick of light ahead.

He stared, blinking, licking his lips. Hope revived and he struggled forward. It *was* a light; there had to be an opening to the outside world. He'd made it! Howards beware!

The shock lent him a burst of energy and he lurched on, half-wading as the water-level went down. The pin-prick swelled; there was daylight beyond. There was a hole, like the mouth of a cave.

The water was down to his calves, his ankles, when he stumbled into the open and pitched forward, almost unconscious, feeling the warmth of the sun on his back.

Little Owl crouched on the hillside, as still and quiet as a stone, watching the hole where the river flowed from the ground. When a naked white man staggered out and fell to earth, he knew it was a sign; but was it good or bad medicine?

It was a strange thing to happen, a once-in-a-lifetime event. At the very least it was a powerful medicine, and he needed to read the sign and decide what action he must take.

He made a cautious approach, descending the slope slowly. The man was alive; he could hear teeth chattering, see chest-muscles heaving.

He reached the man and lightly touched his back; it was as cold as winter ice. He turned him over to see his face... A stranger, the skin gashed and bruised and bleeding. A small man, young.

Eyes the colour of a summer sky flicked open to stare at him. Lips curled back in a defiant snarl. He cursed in the tongue of the white man, proving that though the flesh might be weak, the spirit was still strong.

'Howards! Kill!'

This was a sentiment Little Owl could understand and agree with, and so a good omen. He grunted approval, stood up and waved. Two braves came quickly down the hillside.

They carried the naked man up to where the ponies waited, wrapped him in a horse-blanket and rode swiftly to their village.

A small fire burned in Little Owl's tepee. His woman brought it to life and prepared a thick soup in which floated the tastiest morsels of meat. She spoon-fed the white man and his shivering eased as strength began to return.

'His spirit thrives,' she murmured.

Little Owl sat quietly, smoking his pipe, waiting. The eyes of the white man studied him and Little Owl stared into their depths. He read cruelty there. He was satisfied he'd done the right thing; this man was a warrior sent to aid them.

'Howards,' he said, and mimed the action of cutting a throat.

The white man snarled. 'Death and damnation to all of them!'

Little Owl permitted himself a smile. 'Death for Howards – good!'

The white man tried to stand, but Little Owl pushed him back.

'Later. Eat and rest first. Little Owl is my name.'

'Savage.'

'A strong name. When you are as strong as your name, we will ride.'

'And kill!'

'The valley was once ours. Howards drove us out. Now your enemy is my enemy.'

'When we've finished, you'll have your valley back,' Savage promised.

'That is good.' Little Owl rose and searched among his treasures. He brought a feather to Savage and stuck it in his straw-coloured hair.

'Wear this tail-feather of an owl so that all shall know you.'

Savage finished another bowl of broth and felt his eyes closing. He lay back.

'Sleep well, brother to the Owl,' the Indian murmured, and gestured to his woman who heaped buffalo robes over him.

As Savage rode into Calico, he saw the difference from his first visit, when he'd faced down Garrison, the town boss, and killed him. This time he came in from the west and that section of the town to his right was ashes, fire-blackened adobe walls and silence.

He reached the crossroads before he saw signs of life: Homer Flint taking his ease in an ancient wicker chair on the veranda of the hotel.

Flint didn't recognize him. Savage rode an Indian pony, wearing a blanket around his body and a feather in his hair.

A young man with a swagger laughed mockingly.

'Look what the wind's blown in. I've seen better Indians at a rodeo.'

Savage ignored him till he stepped between him and Homer. The youth's nose wrinkled.

'Jeez, you stink!'

Savage realized he meant the salves Little Owl's wife had rubbed into his skin to heal his cuts and grazes.

He dismounted and hitched the pony.

'I'm here to talk to the organ-grinder, not the monkey,' he said, and placed the flat of his hand against the young man's chest. He pushed, and his critic went sprawling backwards to sit in the dust.

Homer Flint came to his feet in astonishment. He recognized the voice.

'Savage! Jason, behave!'

Jason Flint was on his feet, spitting, drawing his knife. He looked at Homer and hesitated, then reluctantly sheathed his knife.

'What happened to you, Mr Savage?'

'I met some of your Howards.'

'So you got into the valley.' Flint was eager for news. Other members of the clan gathered.

'In, yes. I had some trouble getting out. But I've got what you want and I'll be going back with you to settle something personal. First, I need the balance of my money, to equip myself.'

Homer brought a roll of notes from an inside pocket of his coat, peeled some off and handed them across.

'It's a poor sort of store here.'

'Anything's better than nothing.' Savage nodded to the gathering. 'See you gents later.'

'Join us for a meal at the hotel,' Homer called after him.

The storeman smiled when he walked in with a wad of banknotes in his hand. Since the Flints had arrived, his takings had gone up.

'Clothes,' Savage said, and threw off the blanket.

The storeman's eyes widened when he saw fresh scars and darkening bruises. 'What...? Never mind, I don't want to know.' He measured by sight. 'Small size.' He kitted out his new customer.

As he dressed, Savage said, 'I'll need a shotgun and shells, and a knife.'

'Yes, sir.'

Savage carefully fitted the owl's feather to his hat band, settled the hat on his head and walked back to the hotel.

In the dining-room a select group of seniors sat

eating, together with the young man who had mocked him.

Homer introduced them, one by one, until, at last: 'And this is Jason, who represents the younger members of the family.'

Savage nodded and sat down. Someone had been hunting and the meal was largely freshly cooked meat. After the hotel man had brought in jugs of coffee, Homer got up and closed the door.

Savage gave an account of the Howards he'd seen, their weapons and horses, the layout of the buildings and the guarded entry points to the valley.

Jason wasn't impressed. 'Took your clothes, did they? I wouldn't let any Howard do that to me. I say we don't need this spy any more. I say we can take the valley without him.'

'How d'yuh reckon to get in?' Savage asked mildly.

'Rush them.' Jason sounded almost contemptuous. 'We've got the numbers, and the latest in rifles.'

'And the valley has a narrow entrance at each end – or weren't you listening? The Howards have plenty of hiding places to shoot from – while you'll be in the open.'

Savage turned to Homer. 'It'll need a trick of some kind to get in without a massacre, and I think I know—'

'You think!' Jason's voice held scorn. 'I reckon you've sold us to the enemy. Now you'll lead us into a trap.'

Homer sighed. 'Jason, if there's any more of—'
The young firebrand sprang to his feet, his hand touching the knife at his waist.

'You're wearing a knife, Savage, so show us how good you are. I'm challenging you to a duel!'

8
A Length of Rope

The older Flints sitting around the table in the hotel dining-room froze. The room was silent.

Homer pushed back his chair so he could face Jason directly; his expression was grave.

'You know what that means, Jason. Perhaps you wish to withdraw the challenge?'

'Never!'

Homer's gaunt face looked troubled.

'I'm sorry about this, Mr Savage. What Jason is proposing is a family thing. It is not seemly that he should so challenge anybody outside the clan.'

Savage shrugged. 'He's still growing.'

'I'm afraid you don't understand. The Flint way is this: you each have a knife; you are tied by the wrist to opposite ends of a rope to keep you together; you fight to the death.'

Savage nodded and studied the faces around the table. He reckoned there were some who wouldn't mind if Jason lost. He drawled, 'And after I kill him, what then?'

'If you kill him,' Homer said reluctantly, 'you become an honorary Flint and replace him in the attack on the Howards, and share in ... whatever we find.'

Interesting, Savage thought; something else Homer hadn't mentioned: a share in what?

He looked at Jason. The cocky youngster was grinning. No doubt he believed he was some kind of expert with a knife, but Savage doubted he'd ever killed a man – while he was a waterfront fighter.

He said, calmly, 'I accept the challenge.'

They trooped outside and the remaining Flints joined them. There was a brief explanation and discussion; one man was sent to the store for rope.

Another man remembered an empty lot behind the hotel and they moved there; someone decided it was suitable and the clan formed a square, inside which Savage faced the young rebel.

A few idlers joined the crowd, curious to see what was happening.

Homer measured and cut a length of rope. He tied one end to Jason's left wrist and tested the knot; he tied the other end to Savage's left wrist and tested that. There was just enough slack between them for some manoeuvring. Each man gripped the haft of a knife sheathed at his waist-belt.

The sun was high and Jason moved to get the glare shining into his opponent's eyes.

Savage tested his footing in the dust.

Homer began. 'When I drop—'

But Jason couldn't wait. His knife flashed from its sheath and he lunged forward, intending a quick kill. Savage brought up his knife and steel clashed against steel. Jason darted back; Savage jerked on the rope, pulling Jason off-balance and bringing him within reach.

He slashed high, once, and moved away. Jason hesitated; the blade had cut across his forehead and blood ran into his eyes. Blindly he struck out but Savage was at the full length of their tether, just out of reach.

Jason raised an arm to wipe his eyes clear with the back of his knife hand. Savage danced in and sliced his arm.

Jason winced as the cut stung and tried to get away. Again Savage jerked on the tether, bringing him within reach. Their blades clashed.

Jason was panting, short of breath, his face white beneath the blood, eyes glaring wildly. In a frenzy he hurled himself at Savage, who turned sideways so that the blade only scraped skin from his arm.

Jason stumbled and Savage sliced the knuckles holding the knife.

The young Flint edged back as far as the rope would allow. His air of superiority had gone and he looked desperately around for help.

He saw only hard faces watching him.

'To the death,' Homer said bluntly.

Savage waited, the rope taut between them.

Jason panicked and cut the rope, turned and ran.

Savage recovered his balance, raised his knife-arm as he judged distance, and threw. The blade went end over end and slid into Jason's back till its cold steel touched his heart. He stumbled and fell face down in the dirt.

Homer said bitterly, 'That I should see a Flint run. He has shamed us!'

Savage walked forward and pulled out his knife; he wiped blood from it and cut the rope from his wrist before sheathing it.

Homer stared at him.

'Do the Pinkertons have any idea what kind of animal they've hired?'

'Mr Allan picked me himself.'

The crowd gradually dispersed and Homer took Savage by the arm.

'Come, there are things you need to know now you are one of us.'

They walked back to the hotel and sat alone in the dining-room, behind a closed door, with fresh coffee.

Homer still seemed disturbed by the result of the fight. 'I can only blame his upbringing. A tragedy ...'

Savage asked, 'Why do the Howards hate you so much?'

'The Howards!' Homer Flint might have spat if he'd been outdoors. 'Liars, thieves and murderers. Scum. The start of our feud goes back to the war years; a time close to the end of the war. We – the North – were exhausted, but winning. The rebels were equally exhausted, but losing, and desperate.'

He tasted his coffee and grimaced. He heaped sugar into his mug.

'Some of the worst ruffians formed raiding parties – bushwhackers we called them – vicious killers who slipped behind our lines to kill and rob. The Howard clan formed one of these.'

Homer sipped. 'Let me try to make you see it. Officers owned property or land and, likely enough, had some money in a bank. Troopers came from working homes and depended on wages. They needed their pay, especially if they were family men. Over any commanding officer hung the threat of mutiny or desertion if they weren't paid on time.

'Now imagine a covered wagon rolling south towards one of our advancing armies, carrying a pay-chest, a fortune in coin and paper money. With an escort of a sergeant and six men. In command, my younger brother....'

9
Night Raiders

Lieutenant Ulysses Flint watched the sun descend towards the horizon, and thought, the hell with regulations. He decided to make camp even if darkness was another two hours away. He was weary and sure his men felt the same.

He'd been following a small stream with the idea of camping close to water, so he was a mile or so off his official route. It was unlikely anyone would know if they took an extra rest period to refresh themselves.

Privately he thought it would take a lot longer than an extra hour or two. A month or two wouldn't be enough in his opinion.

The war was in its last stages, the nearest Southern army retreating. As far as he could see the land was empty of life: devastated, crops burnt and animals slaughtered. War, someone had once said, is hell; he and his men knew that from first-hand experience.

They were veterans; young men who looked old, worn down and sick of fighting. They were unshaven, dirty, their tunics torn and bloody. Sometimes Flint wondered if the Union was worth this kind of sacrifice.

When they reached a dip in the land, screened by trees and near the stream, he said, 'Here, sergeant, we stop here. Make camp and post two sentries.'

Flint, though ready to drop, was a responsible officer with a duty to fulfil; to get the chest in the covered wagon through at any cost. His men were few, but experienced; experienced almost to the point of collapse.

'Hobble the horses.'

The wagon-driver doubled as cook and dished up fat bacon with hard biscuits and black coffee. It took an hour before the men began to relax; they were tired, but nerves were shredded.

Flint considered shaving and dismissed the idea; he contented himself with splashing water from the stream over his face. He looked at the sky. Night clouds gathered and soon it would be dark; he estimated the time to moonrise but, even then, light would be spotty because of drifting clouds.

He ordered, 'Change the sentries, sergeant, and get your head down.'

Shadows lengthened. The evening air seemed still and quiet as a grave. Perhaps the sentries dozed, or perhaps the lieutenant did.

He came to with a start and heard a pounding

of hoofs. Then horsemen were in the camp and among the sleeping troopers; a sword flashed, guns blazed. The night was suddenly hideous with Rebel yells and the shrieks of the wounded.

It shouldn't have been so complete a surprise, but Lieutenant Flint didn't have time to enquire what had gone wrong; he reached for his gun, cocked it and aimed. He was sure he hit one of the horsemen before a hail of bullets knocked him backwards.

Raiders, he thought bleakly as he glimpsed his sergeant hurtling through the air after being hit by a charging horse. One trooper fired steadily from under a wagon. Another made a gurgling sound as he drowned in his own blood from a gashed throat.

Raiders ... there were too many of them. He'd heard of guerrillas who slipped behind Union lines, ruthless killers who struck and fled. He guessed there were at least twenty of them; no chance.

One by one his men went down. The crackle of gunfire died away and the raiders dismounted to finish off the injured. These were no worn-out soldiers, but roughnecks who grabbed any chance to kill and rob. He saw one with scalps tied to his belt ... Yankee scalps.

Flint tried to crawl to cover but was too weak to move fast enough. One of the raiders spotted him and walked over, bayonet fixed to a rifle. He grinned like a maniac as he placed one foot on the lieutenant to hold him down, then rammed home

79

the bayonet and twisted it. The body jerked once and was still.

Only when every Northern soldier was dead did the leader of the raiders look inside the wagon to see what they'd got.

As Homer Flint came to the end of his story, Savage looked into his grim and lined face; it would certainly account for the start of a feud.

Homer said, 'Now you see the whole picture. When we take the valley there's going to be a lot of that army-pay left. Northern pay intended for Northern soldiers. Coin and paper-money for an army is more than even Howards can spend stuck out in a wilderness.'

'Sounds good,' Savage admitted, helping himself to more coffee. But he made a mental reservation. Homer had the knack of changing his story to suit each and every situation.

He asked abruptly, 'How d'yuh know all this? You weren't there, and nobody survived who was.'

'I was one of the burial party. I saw the bodies – it wasn't hard to reconstruct what happened. I swore over the body of my brother, that I would avenge him.'

'So how d'yuh know that these raiders were Howards?'

'When the war ended, I travelled south and tracked down the identity of each raiding party. They were notorious, but there weren't many of them – and the only one in that area at that time was made up of Howards.'

Savage repeated, 'So why do the Howards hate the Flints? What have you done to them?'

Homer shrugged. 'Maybe they heard we're after them.'

Savage thought; it sounded a lot more personal than that.

Homer reached across the dining-room table and helped himself to more sugar.

'Enough of history,' he said. 'Here and now, we have to get into that valley. Before Jason interrupted, you had a trick for that.'

'Simple enough. The Howards make money by collecting a toll on each head of cattle they pass through. If we had a herd, even a small one ...'

'I like the idea – simple ideas are usually the ones that work best.' Homer stroked his chin thoughtfully. 'But cattle cost money and I don't have unlimited resources.'

Savage said, 'I've got allies out there, and I figure rounding up a few stray cattle won't bother them at all.'

'Indians, you mean?' For the first time, Homer Flint appeared uncertain.

Savage smiled. 'Why not? They want to kill Howards just as much as you. You ain't figuring to live in the valley afterwards, are you?'

'Hell, no! The sooner I get back to the city the better.'

'That's it, then. You leave the valley to them and you've nothing to worry about.'

There was a knock at the door. It opened and a bearded face peered around the edge.

'We're ready to bury Jason.'

Homer said coldly, 'I know of nobody by that name.'

The bearded man shuffled his feet. 'The young ones want ...'

Homer made a gesture of resigned acceptance. 'Very well, I'll be there – as will Mr Savage.'

He strode out into the fading light and Savage followed them to Calico's Boot Hill, remembering his last visit to this town. He'd killed more than one then.

A grave had been dug, and Jason's body was encased in a coffin hardly more than a wooden crate. Four men stood ready to lower it on ropes. Two grave-diggers leaned on their shovels, ready to fill in the hole.

The Flint clan stood in a group, stiff as pokers, with solemn faces. Savage bared his head, uneasy under their gaze.

Homer wanted this over quickly.

'Dust to dust is the lot of all men, but a Flint goes to his Maker facing the enemy. He does not run away. This man we bury today is not one of us, but a stranger without a name.'

He glowered at the young Flints as the coffin was lowered.

'A man's courage may fail, a Flint's never.'

He turned abruptly and strode away as the grave-diggers began to fill in the hole. One young man, defiant, tossed a handful of dirt on the coffin and said:

'He was my friend.'

Savage imitated his action. 'I did not seek to kill Jason. He challenged me and I defended myself, but it is true that any man's courage may desert him. Even a Flint's.'

Darkness was covering the town as he returned to the hotel, and he decided on an early night.

When Savage came down to breakfast, he found Homer Flint finishing off a meal. He ordered bacon with beans and ate hungrily.

As he reached for a jug of coffee, Flint asked:

'How d'yuh intend to go about this trick of yours?'

'Figure to ride out and talk to Little Owl. He was the one who looked after me. You'd best come too – they'll want to see who they're dealing with.'

Homer hesitated. 'Just the two of us?'

Savage nodded. 'If they see a whole bunch of white men riding towards them, who knows how they might react?'

'Guess you're right,' Homer admitted, but he didn't seem happy about it.

They left the dining-room together.

Savage saddled his pony and adjusted the feather in his hat. Flint brought his horse from behind the store.

'Suggest you wear your gun where they can see it,' Savage said. 'They'll expect you to be armed, but a concealed gun could give them the wrong idea.'

Flint nodded, and brought his holster outside his coat.

Savage rode along easily, beginning to feel almost a Westerner. His companion was uneasy and kept looking around; maybe he'd been reading accounts of Indian raids in a dime novel. Savage was satisfied; maybe he'd learn something about Homer Flint if he kept him unsettled.

'You said this Indian – Little Owl – spoke English.'

'I sure as hell can't speak any native language. He knew enough to get across the idea of killing Howards – something we had in common.'

'How come?'

'I was in no condition to ask questions. Maybe some missionary got at him. Does it matter?'

'I guess not.'

The sun climbed higher and the air heated up. They set a steady pace to avoid ruining their mounts, so it was evening before they sighted the village.

A herd of ponies showed first, watched by a small boy. Then they saw the tepees and heard the barking dogs.

'Don't even look as if you might draw a gun,' Savage warned. 'These people want what we want – and we need their help.'

As they approached the village, warriors came riding out to meet them; half-naked and armed with knives and bows and old rifles. They surrounded the two men.

'Do you see Little Owl?' Flint asked anxiously. 'Is he a chief, or something?'

'I can't see him. From the way the others acted,

84

I figured he must be some sort of medicine man.'

A copper-skinned warrior with a painted face scowled and pointed a lance at them. He seemed suspicious.

Savage began to wonder if anyone would recognize him wearing his new outfit.

'Just keep your hands away from your gun,' he warned Homer again.

Then one of the warriors pointed at the feather in Savage's hat and barked an order; a young man ran back to the village.

After a while, Little Owl came towards them, smiling and calling a greeting; he regarded Savage's companion with obvious curiosity.

Savage said, 'This man is called Flint. He is a sworn enemy of the Howards.'

Little Owl studied his companion, and said, 'Any enemy of the Howards is welcome.' He gestured towards the village. 'Let us eat.'

They moved slowly into the camp, watched by smiling women and excited children. They dismounted and entered Little Owl's tepee and squatted while his woman prepared food.

Little Own said, with satisfaction, 'To kill Howards is good.' Homer nodded.

The food came and they ate, Savage with enjoyment, Homer warily. When they had finished, Little Owl spoke to his wife and she went outside. They waited, the Indian smoking his pipe.

Presently another Indian ducked into the tepee; he was tall and brawny with a paint-streaked face. He squatted beside Little Owl, who said, 'War chief will listen.'

'Can you get cows?' Savage asked. 'With cows, the Howards will open the gate into the valley to let them through.'

'Not let in Indians.'

'No, but can you get cows?'

'Get cows easy.'

Savage indicated his companion. 'Flint has white men, with rifles.'

'Good. Drive in cows – much dust to hide riders with rifles. Indians follow.'

Little Owl turned to the war chief and spoke in his own language. The chief asked questions, and looked searchingly at Flint.

Little Owl addressed Savage. 'Chief asks, "Can we trust this white man? Does he too want the valley?" '

Savage avoided looking directly at Flint. He said, 'Sure you can. He wants only the gold of the Howards. Then he'll leave the valley to you.'

Again Little Owl translated. The war chief grunted, and spoke again.

'He says, "Yes".'

Savage nodded, guessing the chief had said a bit more than that; he guessed the chief was figuring to use whites against whites – then only the Indians could win.

'How long to collect the cows?' he asked.

'One day,' Little Owl answered. 'On the second day kill plenty Howards.'

10
Valley of Death

Michael Howard brooded. When he'd married Naomi, everything had seemed fine; as the husband of the patriarch's daughter he became an important member of the clan. He was big and strong, but he knew he was a slow thinker and Naomi could talk him out of anything.

At first he didn't suspect the reason for the smiles behind his back, but then she quit bothering to hide her appetite for men; when he'd tried to question her, she'd dodged behind Joshua and pretended he was mistaken.

It had been no mistake. He'd had to grind his teeth in private and accept the way she was. Joshua used her to get information out of men travelling through the valley. Michael didn't like it; he resented the situation, but had to put up with it. When he complained, Naomi laughed at him.

It was no better now, even though Joshua had

given him the important duty of gate security. She was, he realized, a natural man-chaser. It was after another row with her that he joined the men at the south entrance to the valley. They kept their smiles hidden and their comments to themselves. Michael was slow to rouse but no one wanted to be on the receiving end when he did lose his temper.

He stared sullenly across the prairie to where a miniature dust cloud rose to the sky. As it grew bigger he stirred; rustlers were bringing in another herd of cattle.

They were raising a helluva lot of dust, he thought, and could hear a thunder of hoofs pounding the ground. They were coming fast, too fast, and he frowned. Why the hurry?

Then he heard gunfire; this bunch was being chased. Suddenly he was startled by wild warwhoops and, through a screen of dust, glimpsed the pursuers. *Indians?*

As they drew closer he saw that the cattle drivers were being chased by Indians on ponies – something that had not happened before. They were shooting arrows which, fortunately, fell short; the rustlers were pushing their horses hard to stay ahead. Slow-thinking Michael felt troubled by this development. He had to protect the entrance, yet …

The cattle – and the horsemen with bandannas covering their faces – were almost at the checkpoint. He hesitated, but not for long. White men had to stick together.

'Open the gate and let the cattle through,' he

shouted; 'We can count them later. Let our guests in too – then shut the gate quick to keep the redskins out. I'm going to tell Joshua and bring more men here.'

He swung into the saddle and headed towards the big house.

Behind him the iron gates opened to allow cattle and riders to surge through together. Once past the entrance, the masked riders turned in their saddles, guns swinging up to aim at armed Howard guards. They shot them down without mercy and the gates remained open.

On the high rock wall above the check-point, the Howard look-out saw only swirling dust and glimpsed the curved horns of steers or the hat of a masked rider.

He barely heard Michael shout for the noise of trampling hoofs and racket of gunshots. He realized the gate must be open as he saw the stampede of cattle into the valley, heading for water; he was shocked to see a few Indians at the rear. Their ponies didn't seem seriously interested in rustled cattle.

There was another burst of gunfire, much closer. The look-out glanced towards the cattle pond and saw a bunch of Howards galloping towards the gate. Something was going on amid all the confusion, and he loosed off a rifle-shot to warn the house.

The single shot alerted Little Owl's war chief, who directed a couple of braves to climb the wall and deal with the look-out.

Homer Flint and Savage were right up there with the leading cattle, shooting at armed guards and trying not to fall under stampeding hoofs.

Homer had a revolver in each hand and a reckless light in his eyes as he rode, pouring lead at every Howard he saw. Savage had his shotgun levelled, but fired once only, to blast a Howard who was directly in his path. The herd didn't stop running till it reached the water; by then, the Flint clan were inside the valley.

Gunfire swept from the shacks near the pool, and Homer's riders charged. The crossfire put everyone at risk and Savage dropped back; he'd never been caught in a blood-feud before and had underestimated its ferocity.

It was a fight with no mercy shown by either side. A Howard man drew a gun and pumped lead as fast as he could pull trigger till it was empty. A Flint shot his man in the back. Both sides were cruel, crafty and as dangerous as mountain cats.

Howards were mostly on foot, defending their homes, with Flints riding in circles around them; it was a killing ground where no quarter was sought or given; the fighting was bitter and aimed at extermination.

There came the whiplash crack of a rifle. Savage's mount stumbled and he slid from the saddle, hanging on to his shotgun. Howard riders had arrived from the north end of the valley. He picked himself up and started to walk, unmolested; perhaps they thought he was one of them now he was on foot.

The fighting moved on, leaving him to cross the battlefield – where Little Owl's warriors were finishing off some wounded Howards.

Savage rejoined Homer Flint who was staring at the flag flying in front of the big house: the Stars and Bars of the Confederation. Savage had never seen him so animated.

'Southern murderers,' he shouted, shaking with rage. 'You shall be avenged, Ulysses!'

A lull came as both sides paused to reload and allow red-hot weapons to cool. Savage looked towards a corral and saw the pony he'd hired in Fremont; this time he might ride back on the mount he'd charged to the Pinkertons.

He glanced at Homer; was he supposed to protect him? Dave Bridger expected 'Smith' to pay for time and expenses on this job. Savage dismissed the idea. Homer had started this so let him look out for himself.

Homer was staring up the slope to the big house. Some of his men had charged up and been shot out of their saddles. He'd underestimated the Howards' defence; the house had been turned into a fortified stronghold.

Michael Howard moved his horse along towards Rattle at a mile-eating lope.

He worried about leaving Naomi, but surely even Flints didn't make war on women? As yet, he had no idea of the catastrophe that had over-whelmed his family.

Returning to the south checkpoint with extra

armed men, he'd been shaken to see that the invaders were not Indians.

'Flints,' growled one of the older men with him, and spurred his mount forward to attack.

Michael had slowed. He was young enough to remember when the name 'Flint' was used to keep children in order. It was a threat from the past, a name out of legend; a treacherous enemy had returned.

Michael was slow on the uptake but realized that one man wouldn't make that much difference; it occurred to him that it could be important to let Mr Christian know about this invasion.

He resented the way Joshua made use of his wife but Mr Christian didn't hide away in a valley. He lived right out in the open, in town, and owned a bank. Mr Christian was someone he could look up to, and admire.

By this time he had been left behind, and he'd made up his mind. He swung his horse about and set off for Rattle, confident he could leave the situation to Mr Christian to deal with. He'd know what to do.

Savage gave all his attention to the house. The important Howards, the ones he had a score to settle with, were inside, and he remembered Calico.

'It's only wood,' he murmured, 'It'll burn.'

'We'd have to get nearer,' Homer said, acutely aware that the number of his fighting men had been cut down.

Savage saw Little Owl watching from a distance and walked over to him. The Indian smiled his satisfaction.

'Kill many Howards!'

Savage agreed, and added, 'The big house has many more. Fire arrows?'

Little Owl gave a low grunt of pleasure. 'Fire arrows, yes!'

He spoke in his own language and half a dozen brawny warriors with bows followed Savage to the cookhouse where he'd eaten previously. He found a can of kerosene. The Indians tore strips from the clothes of dead Howards and Savage soaked the rags in oil. They tied them to their arrows and Savage picked up a box of matches.

They moved up to the big house while the surviving Flints laid down a barrage of lead to cover them. Arrows were notched, bows drawn and aimed.

'The roof,' Savage said, as he struck a match and touched it to oily rags.

The bowmen released their fire arrows one after another; blazing, they soared high to land on the roof of the two-storey building and set dry wood alight. Several small fires started within seconds; the Howards had no chance to douse them.

Smoke billowed in swirling clouds; red and orange tongues of flame merged until it looked as if the whole roof were burning.

Howards ran from the house, shooting as they came. Flints shot back and the fight turned into a massacre; bodies piled up till it seemed that few on either side would survive this bloody battle.

Homer stood four-square, a gun bucking in each hand. Another Flint pulled down the Stars and Bars and set it alight. Savage moved back from a surge of heat; he still saw no sign of Joshua, or Michael, or Naomi.

Watching the end of the Howards, he suddenly remembered what they were supposed to have come for; the pay chest. If it really existed, how would they find it?

He moved up to Homer and tapped him on the shoulder.

'Maybe the chest is hidden somewhere. Leave one of them to talk, or we may not find it.'

Homer grunted something, then nodded, but went on urging those Flints still standing to kill Howards. Then Joshua came storming out of the burning building.

He had picked a moment when the Flints were reloading. He looked every inch the patriarch, dressed in black, his full beard flowing.

'You no good Yankee dog,' he shouted. 'Stop hiding behind your spawn of Satan. Always a cheat, never an honest fight. I dare you to come up here and face me, man to man!'

Homer Flint fumed like a burning fuse. He rose up to his full height and strode towards Joshua like an undertaker keen to bury one more body.

He shouted, 'Robber, child-murderer! I'll kill you with my own hands!'

Behind Joshua the house burst into fresh

flames as rafters burnt through and the roof fell in with an explosion of sparks.

'Die, you bastard!' Homer bawled and drew his hidden revolver.

He fired and his bullet hit Joshua in the shoulder, but the blood-spattered Howard was moving downhill and closing fast; a hand went under his coat and brought out a huge Bowie knife.

'Set a trap for me, will you!'

He lunged at Homer's stomach and ripped him open. Homer gave a dreadful cry and collapsed, and Joshua tripped and fell on top of him.

As their blood mingled, Savage moved quickly to them. He snatched up Homer's revolver. 'Remember me?' he asked.

Joshua lifted his head and peered at him. Savage placed the muzzle of the revolver to his ear and pulled the trigger.

Homer muttered, 'Too late … he's done for me.'

There was a short period of almost silence, broken by the sobbing of a wounded man. The fighting stopped. With both leaders dead, the few survivors stared at each other with dulled eyes. No longer was there anyone to urge them on, and they appeared reluctant to continue a battle that had become largely pointless.

Savage looked around him, and then towards the corral and barn. Two figures moved towards the horses. He frowned. One was Naomi, the other her black maid, and they were carrying a chest between them.

He covered the distance in long strides, and

called, 'Stay right where you are! I want to see what's in that chest.'

The dark-skinned maid looked up and saw him. She froze. Then she dropped her end of the chest and her mouth opened in a long wail.

''Tis the dead come back to haunt us! I see a ghost, Missy!'

She was hysterical and began to shake and continued to wail until Naomi slapped her face.

'Don't be such a superstitious fool, Rebecca! I can see him too, so he's just as real as we are. Though I have to admit I don't understand how ...'

Milton walked bow-legged along the planks towards Dr Jack's place. It was hot again but, despite that, he moved as quickly as his size and weight allowed. Even on an errand of mercy, at Mr Christian's direct order, he didn't like to be absent for long.

He was aware of local men getting out of his way; they were afraid of his strength and the fact that he had Mr Christian's backing. The boss, he thought contemptuously, could buy and sell any of them.

Then he noticed a rattlesnake sunning itself in the dust of Broadway; he averted his gaze and hurried past, his face a shade paler. Milton feared no man, but snakes always gave him the shudders.

A memory returned.... He was being pursued by bounty hunters when his horse put a foreleg in a hole and threw him. Half-stunned, he crawled to the cover of some rocks.

His rifle was under his horse; he had only one revolver and little ammunition, but he reckoned he had a chance if they got careless. There was no fear in him.

He shook his head to clear it, and waited for them to come to him.

The bounty hunters split up to approach from different directions. They crouched low, running from rock to rock; each was armed with a rifle. They worked their way closer, firing alternately.

One shouted, 'The reward says dead or alive, Milton. We prefer dead!'

Chips of rock sprayed around his head. His lips curled back. So what? He'd been in tight corners before and …

That was when a rattlesnake crawled slowly over his boot and he froze in terror. Milton was racked by great shudders; unable to move. This was his worst nightmare; he stopped breathing, paralysed, all his attention on the slow-moving length of mottled brown and orange snake.

He was only vaguely aware of the hunters sneaking closer. It was the reptile that exerted a deadly fascination and held him prisoner; he was like a rigid bar, vibrating under stress.

He heard two gunshots, close together, and the snake glided away.

He stopped shaking and brought his revolver up. He paused, finger on trigger. He saw both hunters fall to the ground and breathed again.

It was easy to see his rescuer had been a military man; although short in height and small of body, he held himself stiffly as if on a parade ground. A cavalry sword was sheathed and he held a carbine.

He nodded to Milton then rounded up the dead men's horses. When he returned, Milton said, 'I owe you.'

'My name is Christian Howard, and I know those two of old. Northern scum.'

As they rode together, Milton began to appreciate his luck. His rescuer owned a bank, and the bank controlled a town. His rescuer could offer protection because he owned the local law.

He stayed to work for Mr Christian, and now he looked after the boss, which was why he didn't want to be away for long.

Mr Christian was in pain and needed his medicine. He reached Doc's place, a small house set back from the street, and pushed open the door.

Dr Jack was taking it easy, feet up and eyes closed. Stupid clown, Milton thought, too old for anything – always sleeping – but there wasn't another doctor in town.

He shook him awake. 'You make a mistake with the boss, and I'll make no mistake with you.'

Dr Jack opened his eyes and stretched; he was too old to let the bodyguard's threat bother him.

'The usual, is it?' He lowered his feet and went to a cabinet.

'Yeah, and hurry it up. The pain's real bad this time.'

Milton was suspicious of all doctors; not one had done the boss any good. It was always the same; something to deaden the pain but no cure. They were useless.

He grabbed the bottle Dr Jack held out and shoved his beringed fingers under the doctor's nose.

'I've put plenty of work your way, so you know what to expect. If this stuff hurts Mr Christian, I'll smash yuh into so many bits that an army of doctors won't put you together again!'

11
The Pay Chest

'Open the chest,' Savage demanded.

Naomi glared at him. 'Why should I? Mind your own damn business!'

'Could be a certain pay chest I've been told about.'

'Could be ...' She gave a short laugh without any humour to it. 'Is that what all this is about? My God ... your friend Flint didn't take you into his confidence, did he?'

'No friend of mine,' Savage said, and thought back. 'My supervisor called him a client.'

'You really are a Pinkerton agent? Rebecca stop shaking like an aspen and open the chest.'

The ebony-dark maid fumbled with a catch and threw open the lid. She backed away when he approached, rolling her eyes and mumbling a prayer.

Savage saw women's clothes, and plunged his hand into the chest, groping deep down. He found only more dresses.

Naomi seemed briefly amused. She filled and lit her pipe.

'Do you fancy a pair of lady's lace drawers?'

Savage gave up. 'So where's the pay chest?'

She sighed, gestured at the bodies lying around, then looked up the hill to the burnt-out ruin.

'If you'll wait till the ashes cool, you can get down to the cellars. *That* chest, and its contents, have possibly survived.'

'Aren't you interested?'

Naomi puffed on her pipe, obviously getting satisfaction from the tobacco.

'I was about to hitch a team to my carriage in the barn, to find out if Uncle Christian has a generous bone in his body.' She sounded bitter. 'Rebecca, stop that keening! Mr Savage, will you please tell her how you escaped from the Devil's Hole. I must admit, I have a certain curiosity too.'

He said, shortly, 'There's a river at the bottom. I was lucky, and swam out.'

'Now, Rebecca, you see Mr Savage is only flesh and blood like me and you.' She turned to him again. 'Perhaps you'll hitch the horses to my carriage and escort us to Rattle?'

'In exchange for...?'

'In exchange for a hot meal. It's a long ride, and Rebecca is a good cook. Which is more than I am.'

The suggestion reminded Savage he hadn't eaten lately, that the feud was over and his client dead. He was in no hurry to go anywhere. The few Flint survivors were already leaving.

He nodded. 'There's a cookhouse by the pool. If you ladies will give me a few minutes, I'll remove the bodies.'

He walked down the hill, where Indians were busy scalping dead Howards. He dragged out the corpses, one by one, and dumped them behind bushes.

Rebecca was soon at work and Savage found that Naomi was right; she was a good cook and he enjoyed pork chops and mashed potatoes followed by sweet black coffee.

'I don't remember seeing Michael,' Savage remarked.

Naomi shrugged. 'Who knows with Michael? He may have been checking the far gate.' She seemed uninterested. 'I find myself dreaming of what might have been. Before the war we had plantations and fine houses and servants, our own way of life ... till scum from the North came murdering and raping and looting. The war spoiled everything.'

'Losers always lose,' Savage pointed out. 'What did you have against the Flints?'

'You will see for yourself.' She pushed back her chair, and Savage followed her outside. He collected a shovel from the barn and they went up the rise to the cooling ashes of the house.

Naomi pointed. 'About here.'

He cleared away grey ash to reveal steps going down, and descended warily.

This cellar was smaller than the one he'd been imprisoned in and obviously held only broken

chairs or worn-out household items. In one corner
was a chest similar to Naomi's, and it felt heavy.
Excited, he dragged it up the steps and into the
daylight. Neither Naomi or her maid showed any
enthusiasm.

He moved the chest clear of the ash and found
it wasn't locked. He opened it to see canvas bags
and bundles of banknotes; he wrenched at a bag
and coins spilled out.

Naomi said in a flat voice, 'I advise you to look
more closely.'

He tapped a coin and got a dull sound. He held
up a banknote to the light and saw that the printing was blurred.

'Counterfeit!'

Naomi said bitterly, 'Damn right it's counterfeit. All of it, every note, every coin – so now you
know why we hate the Flints. They baited a trap
and we fell into it.'

She took a long breath. 'My family was tipped
off about a pay-roll travelling behind an advancing army of the Union. We were in trouble – we
needed weapons and ammunition to drive back
the invaders – and here was a chance to take the
enemy's money to use against them. We couldn't
resist it.'

Savage said, 'Homer Flint told me about the
raid.'

'But he didn't tell you about the Howard who
died in the attack – murdered by Flints. Nor the
fact that when we got clear away with the pay
chest it held only counterfeit money. We'd been

tricked, lured into a trap – for nothing.'

It was obvious to Savage that she was repeating what she'd been told by somebody else.

Naomi continued, 'This was immediately before the war ended. If we'd been wealthy we would have bought the law, but we'd been robbed and cheated and ended with nothing. We were branded outlaws by a Union court and had to run for it. You see now why we hate Flints.'

'Who told you all this?' Savage asked, trying to recall Homer's version of events.

'Joshua, of course.'

Well, it didn't matter now, Savage thought; none of it mattered any more. He turned away.

'Let's get your horses hitched. There's nothing to stay for.'

There were few Indians about, but Little Owl came up to him as he prepared to leave with the two women.

'Valley ours again,' Little Owl said, expressing satisfaction. 'Very good. Chief bringing village here.'

'That's fine,' Savage said, saddling his own horse.

'Savage welcome to visit.'

'Thanks, I'll keep that in mind.'

He rode alongside the carriage, with Naomi driving and Rebecca giving him the eye as they headed for Rattle.

The pain was bad this morning. A spasm racked him and Lew, the barber, lifted his razor and stepped back. Christian Howard took a long deep breath and held it, trying not to scream out loud; his face twisted in sudden agony.

Lew waited patiently. Mr Christian had money and power, but Lew wouldn't have changed places with him for everything he owned. He waited for the town boss to stop shaking so he could finish the shave and escape.

Behind Lew, Milton leaned against the wall, watching the barber. Mr Christian's bodyguard couldn't stop the razor slipping, but he could avenge it. His orders were clear on that point.

'You want your medicine, boss?'

Christian Howard shook his head. The back room of the bank, where he lived, was quiet except for his ragged breathing as he fought to control the pain eating at him. Doctors had done little for him; the current quack supplied laudanum to get him through the night. But he relied on work to survive during daylight hours. Work, and the inflicting of pain on others. Why should he alone suffer?

He relaxed as the spasm passed, and Lew moved in to wield his blade once again. He didn't much like Lew; a sly one, but Archer found him useful.

Christian Howard did not speak; he kept his gaze on the cavalry sword on the wall and brooded over the still confused situation in the valley. First it had been Indians invading; then Flints; now rumour insisted on a massacre. Nothing was sure and he needed to keep a clear head.

Michael had brought the first word, and Christian remembered what happened to bringers of bad news in the old days; but Michael might yet be useful.

Then two guards, who'd been on duty at the north gate, had come in with a small bunch of cattle. And the one buyer in town had grown nervous and left abruptly.

Christian Howard scowled as he brooded. He could smell trouble but was reluctant to move and start over again. He'd grown roots here since the end of the war.

And since his injury he was even more reluctant. He'd wait for news: hard news, not rumour, was what he needed to base a decision on.

He recalled Archer telling him of a Pinkerton in town; to a Southern fanatic any Pinkerton represented Northern-style law. That one had gone down the Devil's Hole ... but Christian's hackles rose at the thought of another coming to Rattle.

Lew finished after a few more strokes and wiped away soap and whiskers. He packed his kit and left.

Christian Howard gripped the wheels of his chair and rolled forward, ready to face the day. Milton fell in behind him.

Snoopers. Just the idea of having a Union spy around upset him. Buy him off, the marshal advised. Perhaps. Or perhaps he would devise something special for the next snooper.

Savage came into Rattle riding behind Naomi's

carriage. She took a back-street to the livery, yet there were still townsfolk abroad, waiting for news. Naomi Howard sat up straight, her horses trotting briskly; Rebecca, beside her, sat with her feet resting on top of the chest of clothes.

He discreetly dropped back, dismounted and led his horse inside the stable. He unsaddled, took up his bags and shotgun and stood in the doorway.

He watched the carriage come to a halt outside the hotel and saw Michael hurry out. He appeared glad to see his wife and she slipped easily into his arms. Together they entered the hotel.

Savage waited a few minutes; he had no wish for a confrontation with Naomi's husband, especially when she seemed to be intent on making up to ensure her own survival.

He booked a room and ordered a bath. From the window he looked out on Broadway and saw she had got it right; there was a rattlesnake sunning itself in the middle of the street.

He went down and took a meal in the dining-room. By then, shadows were lengthening and he was beginning to feel human again. He stood in the hotel porch for a while, watching as men met and talked. Perhaps things were about to change in Rattle.

Then he went upstairs to his room. In the passage at the top of the stairs he found Naomi's maid waiting.

She rolled her eyes and lowered her voice. 'The mistress and Mr Michael – you'd never believe they've been married for years.'

She followed him to the door of his room. 'I'm surplus for the moment ... and you sure enough ain't no ghost. I can do a lot of good for a flesh-and-blood male.'

As he opened the door, she slid inside and stood with her back to him. 'Unhook me, man.'

While he fumbled with the fastenings, she crooned in a soft and persuasive voice, 'I'm from New Orleans, Mr Savage, and who d'yuh think it was who taught Naomi her loving ways? If you're interested I know some variations said to be from Paris, France.'

He discovered she had a yielding figure, a distinctive smell and a way of rubbing herself against him that aroused him quickly.

He pushed her on to the bed, shed his clothes and sprawled across her. After the first explosion of relief, he explored her dusky skin and nest of wiry hair.

She chuckled her satisfaction. 'You sure some kind of man, Mr Savage, so I gives you a friendly hint. Walk careful around Mr Christian; he ain't no lover of city gents from up North.'

She kept him fully occupied till he sank towards an exhausted sleep. Dozing off, his mind wandered to that old pay chest. Had it ever held money? If so, where had it gone? And who had it now?

Kate Fish rode into Rattle as the sun was sinking and shadows were reaching half-way across Broadway. She was a dumpy woman astride a mule and wore a patched shirt, a battered hat and a long leather skirt. The light in her eyes and the set of her jaw would have warned any man she was not here on a social visit.

Eddie, the marshal's deputy, watched her pull up outside Quincey's saloon, dismount and push through the batwings. His only reaction was to be glad he wasn't her unfortunate husband.

Inside the saloon a small group of men were talking quietly, only one or two drinking. They had serious expressions and stopped talking immediately she came in.

In the hush, Kate sniffed. The place was small and the sawdust smelt of stale beer. Quincey, behind the bar, watched her with neither a smile nor a word; he didn't get many female customers.

'Name's Fish,' she said.

One of the drinkers, a homesteader, left his chair.

'Kate! What are you doing here? How's George? Let me buy you a drink.'

'Sarsaparilla.'

Sour-faced Quincey served it and she sipped, looking over the seated men. Some she knew. A few she knew by sight, the baker, the blacksmith. They were all small traders or homesteaders.

She drained her glass and set it down on the counter.

'George is alive, but Dr Jack says he may never fully recover. That's the way it is when Milton hurts someone. As you know, George wasn't the first to try to borrow money from the bank.'

She regarded them without warmth. 'If any of you propose to act, now is the time. I hear the valley Howards are finished, except for Joshua's daughter and her husband. Isn't that what this meeting is about?'

No one contradicted her.

'Christian Howard won't see any more cattle coming through, and he can't sell any more supplies in the valley. Act now, and maybe he'll quit and we can take our town back. This is the best chance we'll ever have – we need to organize and fight now!'

'Against Milton?' Theo, who ran a small café. sounded doubtful.

Her audience shifted uneasily, and there was a marked lack of volunteers to take on Christian's bodyguard. She looked directly at Rattle's blacksmith.

'You've got the muscles.'

'And suppose I took a fourteen-pound sledge-hammer to him? Archer's the law around here and he—'

Scorn dripped like acid from Kate's tongue. 'Christian's hired gunman. I don't accept his kind of law.'

She stared them down. 'How about you, Pope? Without Christian's big emporium, you'll have a chance to grow. You sell guns.'

The storekeeper gave a weak smile. He was called the Pope because he wore a stiff collar and refused to open his shop on Sundays.

'To grow, I need to stay alive.'

110

'It's now or never. I'm not letting Christian's bully-boy ruin my husband without fighting back. Are you with me?'

'Of course, Kate, but—'

She used some unladylike words. 'But nothing! I heard there's a Pinkerton in town. Maybe he'll do something while you talk your way out of it!'

12

Interview with a Cripple

Savage lingered over a late breakfast of bacon and hash browns with coffee. He was taking life easy while he considered what he might do. He should, he supposed, report back to Dave Bridger in Fremont. Yet a memory nagged at the back of his mind, something he couldn't quite put his finger on....

'Mr Savage.'

The voice came from one side and he turned his head to see Rattle's marshal standing there.

'Mr Archer,' he acknowledged.

'Mr Christian requests that you call on him as soon as convenient.'

'Why should I?'

A waitress brought Archer fresh coffee and poured another mug for Savage. The marshal sat down.

'It could be to your advantage.'

Savage sipped the hot brew and Archer waited while he thought it over. Finally, Savage nodded.

'Yeah, why not?'

The marshal stood up and escorted him from the hotel and across the street to the bank. They were about to enter when Naomi Howard came out; she glanced at Savage but walked past without a word.

Inside, one clerk sat behind a counter; there were no customers.

Archer opened a door marked PRIVATE; beyond was a short passage and then another door into a room where three men waited for him.

One Savage recognized as Danser, the newspaper editor. Another was the huge man on bowed legs, Milton, the bodyguard. The third was a small thin man in a wheelchair.

Savage stared. This cripple must be the famous Mr Christian, the man who owned the town and gave the orders. The one everyone feared. He almost laughed.

A grimace that might have been a smile passed across Christian Howard's face; then he composed himself.

'Thank you for coming, Mr Savage. Please be seated. I have a few questions concerning what happened in the valley. Mr Danser will be printing a full story, naturally.'

Danser nodded, peering through steel-rimmed spectacles as Savage sat down. 'Or a version to suit readers of the *Echo*. I remember you from your previous visit, Mr Savage, when you weren't at all helpful.'

Standing behind Savage, Archer said quietly, 'This time I think he'll tell us a bit more about himself.'

Milton didn't say anything at all, just watched closely.

'We heard you're a Pinkerton man,' Archer went on, 'hired by the Flints. Any comment?'

Savage shrugged. 'My supervisor was hired by a man calling himself "Smith". I got the job and, later, this Smith told me his name was Flint. Seems there was a feud going between Flints and the Howards.'

Christian Howard leaned forward in his chair. 'What happened in the valley, Mr Savage? I'm tired of rumours. I want facts.'

Savage was conscious of the marshal just behind him. Even if he did have a wave in his hair and his guns had pearl handles, they still had real bullets in them.

'From what I saw, the Flints joined up with some hostiles to break in. My impression is that there's not many Flints *or* Howards left, so the Indians are in possession. I guess you could say the feud's over.'

'These Indians, could they be shifted?'

'Not easily. First time, I reckon they didn't know any better. They won't be so trusting again, and the valley's easy to defend.'

'And you, Mr Savage? What sort of report will you be filing with your office?'

'That depends....'

Christian Howard's body jerked like a puppet whose strings had been pulled. A grimace crossed his face. Savage looked away; and saw the cavalry sword hanging on the wall.

After a few seconds, Christian regained control and asked, 'Depends on what? Milton can be very persuasive, and Danser can help you frame a suitable report. Archer believes a cash offer is the best way to avoid future trouble. Shall we say fifty dollars?'

'Make it a hundred,' Savage said.

'One hundred, agreed.' He scribbled a note. 'Hand this to my clerk. You're on the team, so remember: you were lucky with the Devil's Hole, but swimming won't do you any good against Milton.'

The bodyguard grinned and flexed his muscles. He stuck one hand forward, fingers curled so that the heads of the iron-nail rings stood out.

'Reckon not,' Savage acknowledged, and then thought: but I expect I'll think of something. 'Got to see about my horse now.'

He walked out of the room and presented the chit to the clerk. With money in his pocket again he left the bank and crossed to the livery; his cayuse had been rubbed down and fed and was ready to go.

'Not just yet, Horse,' he murmured, and stood in the stable doorway watching the town.

Few people appeared to be excited; most were carrying on business as usual. Rattle, despite Christian Howard, was more than a bank and hotel, the emporium and biggest saloon.

The nagging doubt at the back of his mind was becoming clearer when he saw Naomi with Michael; neither seemed happy.

'Hi,' he called. 'Figure I owe you both a drink.'

They stopped. 'No more than that?' Naomi asked.

Michael looked suspicious. 'I ought to smash your face in,' he said, and took a half-hearted swing at him.

Savage stepped back smoothly. 'It's Josh you should blame. He put your wife up to it. At that time I didn't know you were married.'

'That's not the point,' Michael said.

'Not now,' Savage agreed. 'I just had an interview with the boss. I'm on the team, so I've got questions. Let's have coffee someplace – maybe there's money in information.'

'What are you after?' Naomi asked.

'I don't think we have anything to say to you,' Michael said stiffly.

Savage smiled and pulled a dollar bill from his pocket.

'All right,' Naomi said. 'You can buy us coffee or anything else. We're the poor relations and Uncle Christian isn't really interested. There's a diner he doesn't own at the lower end of town. I'd hate to put money in his pocket.'

Savage let her lead the way.

Theo's diner had only six tables but wasn't busy at that time of day. Tables and chairs were rough timber and Savage chose a table away from the window; he sat facing Joshua's daughter and her

116

husband. Theo brought large mugs of black coffee and retreated to his small kitchen.

'I guess Christian's not providing much help for his family,' Savage said.

Naomi looked bitter. 'When we controlled the valley we could have anything we paid cash for. Now ... he suggested I open a laundry, in competition with the Chinese!'

'Michael?'

'He said he had no vacancy for unskilled labour.'

Savage nodded. 'I get the picture. Did you never wonder where he got the money to start up a bank? Things couldn't have been easy after the war—'

Michael snapped, 'Because of you damned Yankees!'

'Not me personally. Things were tough up North too. Let me put a couple of points to you: one, an army payroll goes missing: two, Christian Howard has enough money to start a banking business.'

Michael's face wrinkled in thought, but his expression remained blank. Naomi's eyes glittered like those of a snake. She caught on quickly.

'He was the one! He tipped us off about the pay chest, knowing the money was no good. He used our raid to cover his own theft!'

Michael had trouble with it. 'Where would he get counterfeit money? How could he get access to a Northern army payroll? I don't see ...'

'Why not ask him?' Savage suggested.

Naomi stood up, her face hardening. 'I'll ask him! He owes us, and he'll pay what he owes.' She stalked out of the café.

Michael stared glumly at nothing.

'You going to let your wife take all the risk?'

Michael scowled and clenched his hands; then he got up and went out through the door after her.

Savage called for more coffee. He sat back and enjoyed the fresh brew. That should stir things up a bit, he thought. It would be interesting to see what happened.

He finished his coffee and paid.

Theo, an elderly man with fading hair, asked, 'Has Kate seen you?'

Savage lifted an eyebrow. 'Kate who?'

'Kate Fish. Said she was going to see you ... that's if you're a Pinkerton.'

Word's getting around, Savage thought. 'Not so far,' he answered, and strolled outside.

He paused on the boardwalk to look both ways and noted Archer's young deputy stationed opposite the hotel. A woman wearing a long skirt and battered hat walked up and down outside the hotel porch; a mature woman, obviously impatient. He walked that way and, as he drew near, came under intense scrutiny.

'Are you the Pinkerton?'

'You must be Kate Fish.'

Her eyes sparked. 'I'm Kate. We have a homestead just outside town. George, my husband, got beaten up by Milton.'

'Guess Milton does a lot of that.'

118

'You guess right. You came through the Howard's valley?'

Savage nodded; the set of her jaw told him she was a fighter.

Kate said, 'A lot of us are fed up with the way Christian runs things. I want to break his power, but the men of Rattle are scared of Milton and scared of Archer. We need someone to take the lead.'

'And you need me to lead a fight against a cripple?'

She flushed. 'A cripple with power. I've no money to offer – none of us have – but I love my husband and I'm going to hit back at Christian.'

Savage nodded towards the watcher across the street.

'What sort of man is the deputy?'

'Eddie's a local. He fancies himself as a gunfighter, and models himself after Archer.'

'No law in the county town?'

'Christian controls what Danser prints. Judging by the *Echo* people will believe everything's fine here.' She sounded desperate. 'Someone's got to fight back. You're a man, and you're looking at me the way all men do. Waal, you can have what you want if ...'

'Sure,' Savage drawled, 'let's go upstairs.'

Naomi was furious when she stalked into the bank. That cripple had cheated her all these years, and she'd never suspected. She'd been living an outlaw's life in a forgotten valley; they'd paid through the nose for supplies – while this pathetic wreck sat on a fortune that rightfully belonged to all Howards.

Her rage blinded her. She barged right into Christian's private office without knocking, and ran up against Milton.

Christian Howard raised his voice.

'Never do that again, Naomi. You could get your head blown off.'

She saw then that Archer was also present, and had a gun in his hand. He holstered it when he recognized her.

'You can let her go,' Christian said, amused. 'I can't believe she's a serious threat. Except to my bank balance.'

As Milton stepped away, she rubbed her arms where he'd grabbed her.

'Waal, you can think again. I can expose you any time I like. But that won't be necessary if you pay up – and, by God, you will! Every cent you owe us.'

'Expose?' Christian lifted an eyebrow. 'What does that mean?'

'You know damn well, so don't pretend. You grabbed the real money in that pay chest, all those years ago – and left counterfeit money for our raiders to find. You kept every cent for yourself!'

Archer and Milton stared at her; neither had the slightest idea what she was talking about.

Christian regarded her with a jaundiced eye.

'Who put this idea into your head?'

'Savage. But it's obvious enough now. The

money went missing because you used it to start this bank.'

Christian frowned. 'Savage took my money, and then poisoned your mind against me? Archer, bring him here.'

He watched Naomi as the marshal nodded and left the room.

'I notice you don't deny it,' she said sharply.

'I don't need to justify my actions to common trash.'

'Trash, am I? You're going to pay and—'

He gestured to Milton. 'Discipline her!'

The large bodyguard took a step forward, grinning, and swung his arm. He bunched his hand so the heads of the iron nails that made up his finger-rings stood proud. He struck her once across the face, not really exerting himself.

Naomi was knocked off her feet and ended up across the room, on the floor with her back and head resting against the wall. Her cheek had been ripped open and the bone cracked. Blood poured down her face.

'You bastard!'

There was a tentative knock at the door. It opened and Michael looked in with an enquiring expression.

'Is Naomi here?'

Then he saw her on the floor, tears of pain and rage mingling with the blood.

'He admits it,' she burst out. 'He robbed and cheated us and set Milton on me. If you're any kind of a man, you'll kill him!'

121

Milton smiled and waited for orders. Michael didn't move.

Christian Howard barked a laugh. 'Michael has more sense than to take on Milton.'

His face twisted as a spasm racked him; then he calmed down. 'But you both need to learn the truth. That money is in trust.

'It is not for some vain woman to dress herself in fine clothes, nor to satisfy some male taste for guns and horses. It is in trust for when the South rises again!'

On the floor, Naomi saw the fanatical gleam in his eyes, and spat out blood.

'You're insane, you mad bastard!'

13

Alarm and Confusion

After Kate left, Savage dressed and stood by the window, watching Broadway. Rattle, he suspected, was about to have an interesting time.

He saw Michael help Naomi along the boardwalk and remembered from his previous visit that the doctor's surgery was in that direction. Savage remained unmoved; to his mind they should have known what Christian was like.

He clipped his big Bowie knife to his waistbelt, picked up his shotgun and went down the backstairs. He walked quietly towards the lower end of town and entered a small general store that Christian did not own.

'I'll take two boxes of shotgun shells,' he said.

Pope looked curiously at him, and brought the shells from behind a counter. 'Reckon Kate talked to yuh – no charge for those.'

Savage waited just inside the store, in the shade, looking out. He saw Archer come from the

123

bank and cross to the hotel; he was stepping lively, long hair down to his shoulders, one hand touching the pearl handle of a revolver.

Pope joined him at the door, and Savage said:

'No reason for Mr Christian to stay in Rattle now the valley's closed. Could be room for small men to grow, if the town survives.'

'Some of us were here before he arrived. We'll be here after he leaves.'

Archer came out of the hotel and went into the livery; when he left there, he stood a moment looking up and down Broadway, then went into the Last Round-up.

Christian's saloon was big with a gaudy front. A few minutes later, a dozen drinkers hurried out, hitching at gunbelts. They split up to quarter the town.

'Some of those are rustlers' friends,' Pope said. 'If it's you the marshal's hunting, you'd better slip out the back way.'

Savage nodded and left. Outside the back door he sprinted along a dusty alley to a derelict building and crouched behind a water barrel wedged into the doorway. A pursuer came part way along the alley and gave up.

Savage bared his teeth in a fierce grin. These people could no doubt track a man through the wilderness; but he was a street fighter from the big city. He doubted he'd have much difficulty eluding the searchers.

He waited till he was unobserved, then darted through the rear door of the hotel. He moved like a cat along the passage to the hall. The hotelman was standing just inside the front door, watching the hunters.

Savage jabbed a stiff finger in the small of his back.

'Looking for someone?'

The hotelman turned and recognized him; the colour left his face. 'You...!'

'Me,' Savage said innocently, and fished in his pocket for a few dollar bills. 'Figure to pay my debts – I'll be going shortly.'

As the man grabbed for the money, Savage said casually, 'Did you hear Mr Christian may be leaving town? Reckons to re-open his bank in the next state.'

The hotelman's jaw dropped. 'He wouldn't do that!'

'You'll be all right, then – it's just a rumour.'

Savage ran upstairs to his room, shoved his saddle-bags under the bed and opened the window. No one was looking up, so he climbed on to the ledge and swung himself up on to the roof. He lay flat, listening.

He heard the hotelman sound the alarm. Archer's voice. Footsteps on the stairs and the door slammed open.

'Not here now.'

The search continued but nobody thought to look up. Savage waited for Archer to leave, then swung inside again and padded quietly downstairs and next door to the livery. He saddled his horse and led her out the back way. The stable-

125

man was absent, probably hunting him.

A small boy playing with a dog spotted him and Savage flipped him a dollar piece.

'Hi, son, this cayuse needs exercise. Ride her out of town for a while, circle around and rub her down when you get back. You needn't hurry.'

After the boy rode away, Savage waited in deep shadow, listening to Christian Howard bawl out his tame marshal. It seemed Archer should have caught him before now.

Savage used another back alley to get behind the blacksmith's shop. Here there was a stack of old iron to hide him.

Boots clattered. A long shadow stretched across the ground. 'You look that side, Ben and I'll—'

A tall man in a leather apron and carrying a hammer said angrily, 'Get out of here! Iron's worth money to me, you thieving swine.'

'We're not after your iron! Archer's offering ten dollars a man to find this guy – twenty to the man who grabs him.'

'Waal, there's nobody here but me,' the black-smith said, 'and I'm working, so clear off.'

The hunters moved on and the smith went back to his anvil, ignoring Savage. He waited a few minutes, then followed after the hunters till he came to Wing Fat's laundry.

Chinese workers registered surprise when he walked in; one young girl giggled and hid her face.

Wing Fat appeared beside him, smooth and smiling. He obviously remembered Savage from his previous visit to Rattle.

'Marshal hunt you, yes?'

'He's got himself a pack of brawlers from the Last Round-up.'

Another Chinese murmured something to Wing Fat, who picked up a loose smock and dropped it over Savage's shoulders; he slapped a wide-brimmed straw hat on his head.

'Bend over the wash-tub – keep your face down,' Wing Fat hissed as a couple of roughnecks looked in, staring around suspiciously.

Their gaze passed over Savage because they couldn't imagine him as a laundry worker.

After they'd gone, Savage kept his disguise; with his shotgun out of sight under the smock, he shuffled along the boardwalk, and not one of the searchers challenged him.

When he reached the town jailhouse, he walked inside.

Eddie, the deputy, looked up from behind the desk.

'What d'you want?'

Savage smiled coldly and brought up his shotgun, both barrels cocked.

'Figured I'd be safe here for a while. You've probably got some idea of what this can do at short range, and that's if I fire only one barrel. So stay quiet and march into a cell and I'll lock the door.'

Eddie didn't argue when Savage lifted the revolver from his holster and picked up the keys to the cell doors.

'This is your chance to enjoy a short nap while I watch the jail for you.'

127

'Archer won't like this,' Eddie warned.

'Archer won't have a job once Christian leaves.'
Eddie stared blankly. 'Christian leaving?'

'What would he stay for? With the valley closed
to him and no cattle buyers in town his bank is no
longer necessary.'

'Hell!'

'If you're a good boy, Eddie, maybe the new
town council will appoint you as marshal.'

Savage locked him in and shed his straw hat
and smock. He borrowed the deputy's Stetson and
sat just inside the doorway, hat tilted forward to
hide his face. From beneath the brim he watched
the searchers wear themselves out.

Presently a cry went up. 'His horse has gone!'

There was a rush for horses and the street was
cleared rapidly. Archer returned to the bank and
Broadway quietened down.

Savage took up his shotgun and walked along
the shady side of the street until he reached the
office of the Rattle *Echo*. He pushed the door open
and went in.

Danser was stooped over, setting type; he
glanced up casually.

'I heard you'd left town.'

'Not yet – I have some unfinished business. Got
a story for you if you'll just step along with me.'

The editor straightened up, adjusted his spectacles and reached for a notepad and pencil.

'Just tell me.'

'Always thought you reporter fellers were keen
to get news at first hand.'

'A myth.'

Savage brought up his shotgun, already cocked. 'One barrel or two?'

Danser sighed. 'You know, you're a pain. Where to?'

'Doc's place.'

'All right.' Danser walked along the planks with Savage behind him to the small house with the sign: JACK WARD M.D.

He pushed open the door. 'What's happening here?'

Dr Jack scowled at him. 'As you're apparently blind, I'll tell you. I'm stitching up Mrs Howard's face.'

Savage saw she had a whiskey bottle in her hand, and nodded.

Michael glared at the newspaperman. 'Milton hit her – are you going to print that?'

Naomi mumbled, holding her face, 'At Christian's order.'

Danser put away his notebook. 'You know I can't.'

'What'll you do when Christian leaves?' Savage asked. 'D'you think the people of Rattle will still want you here?'

'Who said he's leaving?'

'There's a rumour going the rounds. There must be something in it.'

Danser hurried out and Savage strolled after him. He paused under a red-and-white striped pole. Lew stood in the doorway watching him.

In Savage's experience, a barber collected and

retold all the gossip in town. He asked, 'Is it right what I've heard? That Mr Christian is planning to close his bank and leave Rattle?'

Lew started. 'First I've heard of it.' He seemed troubled by the idea and Savage moved on to the Last Round-up.

He pushed through the batwings; Christian's big saloon was empty apart from a couple of old-timers at a corner table.

The bartender looked as if he'd seen a ghost.

'I thought you ...' He glanced down at Savage's shotgun and changed his mind. 'I've forgotten what I thought. Will you take a drink on the house?'

Savage shook his head. 'I'm not much of a drinking man. I was just passing and wondered if you'd heard yet: Christian's quitting.'

'So? I'll still be here, and men aren't going to quit drinking.'

'Maybe not, but what will they use for money? Are you going to give credit?'

While the saloon keeper was thinking it over, Savage crossed the street to the emporium, the biggest store in town and owned by Christian Howard. It was empty except for a few women.

Savage asked, 'How's business?'

'Slack. No cattle coming through; no buyers in town. D'you have any idea what Mr Christian might intend?'

Savage smiled.

Sweat trickled down Christian Howard's contorted face. He could not remember being so frustrated and screamed in rage:

'Where is Savage? I want him here, *now*! Why does nobody do what I tell them to do? I want to flay the skin off his bones! I want ...'

He lay back in his chair, exhausted.

The temperature in Rattle was rising, and the clerk in the outer office noticed more than one snake soaking up the sun. He thought he'd rather face them than enter the inner sanctum at that moment. Mr Christian's voice penetrated wood and stone.

Christian felt as if acid were eating away his stomach lining; each visitor to the bank brought a fresh rumour. Only Milton, standing behind his wheelchair, appeared to be unaffected.

'You – Danser – get out a special edition. Deny this nonsense. Of course I'm not leaving here. This is my town and I won't be driven out by lies!'

'Yes sir, right away.' Danser was glad to leave, mopping his face. It was Christian's uncertain temper that made him sweat; the boss was an expert in punishment.

'You, Archer, call yourself a lawman and let this Yankee kid run rings around you? I want him in this office. I'm going to let Milton play with him. You'd like that, wouldn't you, Milton?'

The bodyguard grunted.

Archer sighed. 'You're playing a dangerous game, Mr Christian. If Savage really is a Pinkerton, as now seems likely—'

Christian screamed at him: 'I don't want to know!'

131

'—and if anything happens to him, you'll have a whole pack of them descending on your neck.'

'I don't care!'

'Besides, you ripped open a woman's face and Doctor Jack isn't going to keep quiet about it — *he's* not in your pocket. Ordinary folk don't respect a man who picks on a woman.'

'Ordinary folk, why should I give a damn for any of them? I own this town, and if they don't like my little ways they can leave.'

'If many do, and wag their tongues, you're likely to get a federal lawman investigating.'

'Federal rubbish! I don't recognize any law passed by those Union upstarts.'

Archer shrugged.

14
Trouble With Women

Savage looked across Broadway from the window of the baker's shop. He chewed on a crust of bread given by the baker's wife, while her husband slept in the back room.

He saw Danser leave the bank and walk towards his printing office. He waited, frowning; where had Archer got to?

Outside the heat made the air shimmer while not the slightest breeze disturbed the dust. Before long the saloon brawlers would be back, after discovering he was not riding his horse; and then it would be difficult to make any kind of move.

He decided to accept the risk. He crossed to the bank and found the clerk alone.

'Savage to see Mr Christian,' he said politely.

The clerk's eyes opened wide and he moistened his lips with his tongue. He slid sideways.

'I'll tell him you're here.'

Savage gestured with his shotgun. 'There's no

need for that. Just lead the way.'

He followed the clerk along the passage to a door; the clerk knocked and opened it. Savage edged him aside and walked in, his gaze concentrated on Christian Howard, and Milton standing just behind the wheelchair.

He was about to kick the door shut when he felt the pressure of a revolver muzzle against the back of his skull.

'Stand very still and I shan't have to blow your brains out.' The voice of Archer breathed down his neck. 'It makes a mess, and Mr Christian prefers everything neat and tidy. Milton, take his gun and knife.'

The bodyguard swaggered towards Savage on short, bowed legs, grinning broadly. Without warning he slammed a fist into his stomach. Savage doubled over and hit the floor.

Milton picked up the shotgun and Bowie knife and handed them to Archer.

Savage lay on the floor, struggling to breathe. He heard shouting outside, then a gunshot.

'What's that?' Christian demanded. 'You'd best see to it, Marshal. Milton can do what's necessary here.'

Kate Fish was exasperated. The group over in Quincey's was smaller than before and composed mostly of homesteaders. The townsfolk seemed even more nervous now that Savage was being actively hunted. They were drinking more too.

She held a .22 hunting rifle and waved it vigorously.

'Call yourselves men! The Pinkerton's locked the deputy in his own jail, lured Archer's hired gunmen out of town and gone into Howard's Bank alone. What more d'you want? This is your chance to help free yourselves of the blood-sucker!'

Someone at the back muttered, 'He seems to be doing all right on his own.'

'Too well! Suppose he shuts the bank right down. What do we do then?'

Another shifted uneasily. 'If he fails, Christian will insist on buying us out – at his price.'

'You expect him to do all your fighting for you?' Kate spat in disgust. 'All right then, I'll do the fighting. You want a woman to show you how? Have I got to go out there alone?'

She stalked towards the batwings and one or two men followed, looking sheepish. The rest dragged after her, reluctantly, out of Quincey's and into the heat and dust on Broadway.

They moved slowly along the shady side and paused as hoofbeats sounded. The hardcases from the Last Round-up were returning, and they looked hot, sweaty and short-tempered. Their self-appointed leader led the mare on a rope, with a young boy in the saddle, his hands tied.

The burly man with the dark stubble glared around and demanded, 'Who owns this kid?'

The boy spoke up. 'I told you before, I was only exercising her.'

The man cursed and quirted him across the face. 'Shut it!'

Kate raised her rifle and squeezed the trigger;

135

his hat sailed away. 'Lift that quirt again and I'll kill you.'

'You bitch! This kid led us a chase and—'

'I know you, Butch – a bully and a coward!'

Townsmen and homesteaders closed ranks behind her. The crowd from the Last Round-up got behind Butch, hands gripping gun-butts. Kate and Butch glowered at each other.

'Let the boy go,' Kate said.

Butch laughed. 'Think you can make me?'

An ugly situation was developing, with neither side willing to retreat.

Then a new voice drawled, 'Sure got some real tough *hombres* here, picking on a kid. Reckon they'll start running when a couple of women pick on them. A right bunch of cowards.'

Naomi Howard took her place beside Kate. She wore a fancy red gown cut low in front and held a big Colt .45 in both hands.

But it was her face that held them; the stitches were red and angry.

'Looks like you need a shave, Butch. I'll borrow a razor from Lew if you'll let me have a go.'

Rebecca, her maid, pushed in front, her dark skin enhancing a tight black dress. She chuckled as she lifted her skirt to reveal a froth of white lace; and whipped out a knife.

'No need to wait. I keep this sharp enough to shave a man since I can't abide whiskers in bed ... reminds me of the last time my hand slipped. But you don't want to know about that....'

She glided forward like a hunter stalking her

prey, the thin blade flashing in the sunlight. Butch edged his horse back.

Rebecca cut the boy free and slashed the rope holding the mare.

Naomi said, 'You, boy, return that horse to the livery.'

'Yes, ma'am. Right away, ma'am.'

As he trotted away, Kate kept her rifle centred on Butch. 'Looks like you're finished, feller. Why don't you quit?'

Stubbornly, Butch declared, 'Not till I know where Savage is hiding.'

Kate tugged the brim of her battered hat lower to shade her eyes. 'Hiding? That's more your style, isn't it?'

Butch said, 'If you know something, spit it out.'

A male voice interrupted, carrying along Broadway.

'What's going on here?' Archer came walking briskly from the direction of the bank, holding a shotgun. 'Who fired that shot? And where's Eddie?'

'We were chasing Savage—'

'Forget Savage. He never left town,' Archer said curtly. 'He's in the bank.'

Butch walked his horse towards the boardwalk, cursing.

'Hell, all for nothing – in this heat. I need a drink.' His gang followed, hitched their mounts and pushed into the Last Round-up.

Archer repeated, 'Who fired that shot? You, Kate?'

'He hit a young boy with a quirt.'

'Waal, put that gun down. It's over now.'

Kate lowered her rifle, but contradicted, 'It's not over. If Savage—'

'Savage is safe in Milton's hands. D'you fancy his chances?'

'If he doesn't report in,' Kate said doggedly, 'you'll have another Pinkerton – maybe more than one – on your neck.'

Archer ignored the comment. 'You, Naomi – a Howard – should have more sense. Remember whose side you're on. And keep your maid under control.'

Naomi began to fill her pipe. 'I'm not on Christian's side, after he set Milton on me.'

Archer turned to the third woman. 'Rebecca, I'm warning you. Stop waving that knife around or I'll throw you in jail.'

The black woman rolled her eyes heavenward. 'Along with your deputy? No thanks!'

'Eddie? In jail?'

'That's right, Marshal,' Kate said sweetly. 'Savage thought he'd be safer there.'

Archer swung about and left abruptly, heading for the jailhouse; the townsmen drifted away and Kate, Naomi and Rebecca looked at each other and burst out laughing.

As the door of Christian's office closed behind the marshal, Milton kicked out and Savage rolled with it.

The bodyguard smirked. 'He's shamming, boss.'

Savage stayed on the floor, resting quietly against a wall, getting his strength back. It was not difficult to put on an injured expression.

'What was that for? I thought we were on the same team.'

Christian had regained his calm now he had Savage helpless. His smile was that of a cat playing with a mouse. 'That was because you put ideas into Naomi's head. Because you told lies about me.'

Savage protested, 'You've got it backwards. Naomi told me. And I've heard rumours too. I was trying to find who started them.'

'So why sneak in here, armed to the teeth?'

'Sneak in? I asked your clerk to announce me. I got curious about Naomi's story is all, and was going to ask you what really happened.'

'Ask me?' Christian gripped the wheels of his chair. 'Why me?'

'I've heard Homer Flint's version of the raid, how you Howards ambushed a pay wagon and stole the money. Then I heard Joshua's version, how the Flints cheated them by loading the pay chest with counterfeit money ... and I wondered, what's your version?'

Christian parried, 'Why should I have a version? I wasn't anywhere near the wagon when it was stopped, or afterwards.'

'How about before?'

Savage hauled himself upright and leaned against the wall, watching Milton. He'd got his breath back. Now he flexed his muscles.

'With hindsight, it's obvious the money wasn't aboard the wagon when it was ambushed. Someone had already removed it and replaced it with counterfeit – the raid covered the switch so it wouldn't be noticed. And Joshua and his clan got the blame.'

Christian stared at him. 'Is that what you think? Bearing in mind that no one can prove anything after all the time that's passed.'

Milton seemed bored, waiting for his boss to give the order that had to come.

'It's not a question of proof. I think Naomi's probably right. Look at it this way; the money went missing – you started a bank. Put like that it's clear enough.' Savage pointed to the wall. 'Is that sword yours?'

Christian nodded.

'I'll guess it belonged not to some guerrilla raiding behind the lines, but to a cavalry officer in the regular Confederate army. As an officer, you'd have access to information denied unofficial raiding parties.'

Savage put on an admiring expression. 'It couldn't have been easy, even then. Let's assume that, somehow, you got hold of a batch of counterfeit money....'

Archer turned the key in the lock, releasing his deputy.

'I warned you not to get over-confident.'

Eddie's young face was sullen. 'He took me by surprise – had a shotgun real close. It'll be different when I meet him face to face. Then I'll—'

Archer shook his head. 'It'll never happen, Eddie. Savage is the sort who makes sure he always has an edge. He's dangerous, so stay away from him if you want a future. He's out of your class. Now get your gun and we'll start patrolling.'

'I heard a crowd and … who got shot?'

'No one. Kate scared Butch, is all.'

'Kate Fish?'

Archer nodded. 'Kate and Naomi Howard – and her maid – got together and seem dead set against Christian. Are you up to shooting down a woman in public? Suppose you kill one of them. Reckon you'll be running for town marshal? Or running one step ahead of a lynch mob? You're a local – how d'you read them?'

Eddie blinked rapidly. It was not a question he wanted to face.

'Is it right Mr Christian's leaving?'

'Not willingly,' Archer said drily. 'Imagine you're facing three women, two armed with guns, the other with a knife. What are you going to do? Think about it.'

Eddie didn't want to think about it. He just couldn't imagine it. His face was clouded as they walked down Broadway, side by side. The crowd had dispersed, but one or two idlers watched from outside a saloon. The air was stifling, hot and dry, and dust stirred beneath their boots.

'Take it slow and steady,' Archer advised. 'This is no time to make the first mistake.'

They continued to the bank and Archer paused

in the doorway. It seemed ominously quiet, like the lull before a storm.

'Milton's got Savage in there,' he said.

'Good!' Eddie's suppressed fury showed in his eyes. 'I hope he breaks a few bones.'

Archer looked across the road. 'You'd better pray those women don't try to interfere. Or work out how you're going to stop them.'

Eddie stared at three figures on the opposite boardwalk.

Kate, Naomi and Rebecca stood together, talking quietly and watching the bank. Naomi was smoking her pipe. Each woman remembered her encounter with Savage as they waited, listening, wondering what was going on inside.

15

The Third Version

'Got hold of?' Christian Howard echoed the words as if they amused him. 'Our Confederate government supplied the counterfeit, as part of our war strategy to weaken the North. It was left to me to devise ways of getting it into circulation.'

Savage leaned casually against the wall, flexing his muscles and watching Milton.

'But you still had to make the switch, under the noses of Union soldiers.'

Christian had lived with his secret for too long. He wanted to claim credit for his cleverness. And Savage wasn't going to live long enough to repeat anything.

'I wasn't a cripple then and we were close to the end of the war, though nobody realized just how close. It was a time of confusion, armies surging this way and that as opportunity offered, regiments overrun and patrols lost. No one could be

sure where the front line was, or if there was one.
I was near a Union camp with a carpet-bag filled
with forged notes and coins, trying not to look
conspicuous. And then the unthinkable happened.
A Union army officer came to me....'

Christian Howard wore civilian clothes, patched
and none too clean; he hadn't shaved for a couple
of days. He sat on a bench at a table at the back of
a saloon used by soldiers of a Northern army. The
fighting had moved on and nobody, he hoped, was
looking too closely at the dud money he was passing.

He sat with a small glass of beer in his hand,
but sipped rarely. He was tensed up and needed
every nerve alert.

He was small for his age, and lean with it, and
he kept one foot pressed against the carpet-bag
beneath the table. The saloon was smoky and
smelly, some of the soldiers half drunk.

A tall Union captain sat down opposite him and
they watched each other across the table.
Christian felt a tingle along his spine.

'Drink up,' the captain said. He had a neat
moustache.

'I've had enough, but I'll buy you one.'

Christian's offer brought a faint smile to the
Northerner's lips.

'Like you, I've had enough.' He dropped a
banknote on the table between them. 'One of
yours, I think.'

Christian glanced down, and began to sweat.

The captain lowered his voice and leaned closer. 'If you've more of the same, we can help each other.'

Christian sat very still. His only weapon was a hidden knife but if he pulled it his chances of getting out of the saloon alive were as slim as the blade. A knot formed in his stomach.

'What d'you mean?'

'The war's as good as over and it doesn't matter who wins – soldiers get discarded when peace comes. It's time to look out for number one.'

The captain stroked his moustache. 'A stone's throw from here, a payroll is being made up for one of our forward armies. The money will be locked in a standard-issue wooden chest. As you can calculate, pay for even a small army amounts to a fortune.'

He pushed the forged banknote across the table.

'Now, if you can provide enough of these – with coin to make up the weight – we can do business. I've already got my hands on another chest. We switch ours for the one with the good stuff and split fifty-fifty.'

Christian took a sip of beer, glancing around. The saloon was noisy and nobody was taking any notice of them. He could kill two birds with one shot: get the Union army to distribute the counterfeit for him – and take the North's money to buy arms for the South.

'You make it sound easy.'

'It will be, providing nothing goes wrong. Once

145

the money's locked in the chest, it'll be loaded aboard an army wagon. The wagon is in a stable, ready for a daylight start.'

Christian was so excited he had difficulty in breathing; it felt as if his ribs were tightening about his lungs.

'Guards?'

'Two soldiers, and both are men who like a drink. That's easily provided.'

Christian deliberately breathed hard and long till he filled his lungs.

'Let's do it.'

They emptied their glasses and he picked up the carpet-bag from under the table.

The captain said, 'Wait,' and forced his way to the counter to buy a bottle of cheap whiskey. They went out into the night air.

A moon was riding high, dodging between clouds. Bawdy singing echoed from saloons and a few men wove an unsteady way back to camp. Christian was taut as a bowstring; had these Union soldiers no discipline?

The captain led him into a shadowed yard where a horse and buggy were tied to a post. He threw back a canvas to reveal a chest.

'Load your stuff into this. I'll gift my bottle where it'll do most good.'

He disappeared into a pool of darkness and Christian waited, fully alert. A trap? Minutes passed and nothing happened. He opened the chest aboard the buggy and began transferring bundles of banknotes and bags of coins. He

146

worked carefully to avoid noise, and closed the lid.

Someone, he noted, had put a spade beside the chest and he wondered about it.

His pulse was racing and his heartbeat sounded as loud as a drum, but no one bothered him. The night remained still and quiet apart from an occasional drunk stumbling back to quarters.

When the captain returned, he inspected the chest and locked it. His teeth flashed in the dark and he consulted a pocket watch.

'We'll allow them an hour. For the moment, I'm their favourite officer.'

He spoke in his normal voice and Christian began to relax. Who was going to challenge a Union officer here?

Time dragged. A few more soldiers passed by. The captain smoked a cigarette and looked again at his watch.

'All right, we'll try it.'

He took the horse by the bridle and led the way out of the yard. Christian followed. When the moon went behind a cloud it was dark enough to make him careful where he placed his feet.

It was not far to the stable, and when the horse stopped the captain fed it lumps of sugar. Christian waited, sweating. The captain walked into the stable and Christian counted the seconds until he returned.

'Both sleeping. Let's get our chest inside.'

There was a handle at each end and they lifted the chest off the buggy and carried it into the stable. Horses watched them but did not set up a disturbance.

'Here.'

They set the chest down beside an army wagon. Christian heard one guard snoring; the other lay face down. The whiskey bottle was empty.

The captain climbed on to the wagon and shifted the pay chest. Christian lowered it to the ground; it was a bit heavier than theirs containing the counterfeit.

He lifted up the replacement and the captain shoved it further back, out of sight.

Between them they carried the pay chest outside and put it in the buggy. The captain climbed into the driving seat and picked up the reins. Christian got up beside him. The captain flicked the reins and they drove slowly away.

'Waal, that wasn't too difficult was it?' he asked, with a sly smile. 'Sit tight – I don't fancy anyone will stop us now.'

He followed a faint track out across the empty land, past burnt-out farmhouses and scavengers feeding on the remains of slaughtered animals. A mile or two further on, where the land dipped to form a hollow, he drove into a clump of trees and stopped. He cocked his head, listening.

Christian waited. He was sure that treachery was intended and was ready for it. Now he had only one man to deal with he felt calm and confident, and he moved decisively when the captain drew a pistol.

One arm knocked the captain's hand away so

the bullet flew skywards. A thin-bladed knife came down his sleeve and into his hand. The captain tried to dodge; too late, the blade slid between rib bones to the heart. He dropped his pistol and toppled from the buggy....

Christian Howard stared at Savage and smirked.

'Does that answer your questions? I buried the chest and the captain with it and marked the spot. Even in wartime it was too risky to travel far with it.'

Savage kept Milton under observation from the corner of his eye. The bodyguard was leaning against a wall, bored and waiting, flexing his hands.

'And the raid?' Savage asked.

'Naturally we had a system for informing the guerrillas where to strike. I tipped off Joshua's party about the wagon, and they succeeded brilliantly.'

'Succeeded in covering your tracks?'

'Yes. After the wagon was held up and robbed, if anybody worried where the money chest went, that was it. The perfect cover.'

'Except that Joshua killed a Flint and Homer started to look for any Howard to take his revenge on.'

Christian frowned. 'That came later. I had intended, of course, that the money should be used to buy weapons and ammunition for the South. The war ended too quickly for that ... I waited a few months and went back with a horse and cart and dug it up. It was then I moved to this two-bit town where nothing much happens and started this bank.'

'And I suppose you invited Joshua to settle in the valley?'

'Rustlers were already using the valley to bring cattle north. Bringing in Joshua and charging a toll was an obvious move. I'm still here, and the money's still here. In trust for when the South rises again.'

Savage's lip curled. In trust for the South – the man was a fanatic.

'Seems a pity you were crippled, then.'

Christian shrugged. 'A drunken cowboy shooting up the town. A wild shot killed my horse and it fell on me.'

'What happened to the drunk?'

'Milton killed him – as he will you. I've lived in pain for years and no Union spy is going to wreck my plans.'

A spasm crossed Christian's face. 'It still give me pain and the doctors say it always will. And you helped the Flints, you wrecked my operation in the valley, so I'll gladly teach you the meaning of pain. Milton, my sword!'

Savage knew he could wait no longer. He sprang at the cripple, but Milton anticipated his move, and there wasn't room to avoid him.

The bodyguard balled his right hand, iron rings outermost, and clouted him on the side of the head, drawing blood. Savage fell, hitting the edge of a small table that went over, spilling papers.

Milton drove a boot into him and sharp pain shot up his leg. He began to crawl away as Milton handed the cavalry sword to Christian. He wanted to reach the door.

The banker swished the blade through the air. 'Good Southern steel, Mr Savage. With it, I can slice you thin as jerky and enjoy doing it. But not just yet. You must suffer first.'

A fanatical light shone from his eyes. Spittle drooled from his lips.

The bodyguard said, 'Let me, boss.'

'Yes, hurt him, Milton. Break some bones, stamp on him. I want him to live in permanent agony, the way I live … so take care you don't kill him!'

16
Death Rattle

Eddie rolled a cigarette, struck a match and inhaled deeply. Broadway was oven-hot and airless. The quiet, the waiting, were getting on his nerves. He was young and aspired to be a gunfighter but, right now, doubts were creeping in.

He glanced sideways at Tom Archer. The marshal was still as a statue, apparently relaxed, listening. Only his eyes moved, darting here, there, everywhere.

Across the width of the street, three women stood on the plankwalk, talking quietly. Eddie sucked on his cigarette. Would they start anything? If they did, could he shoot one of them? Doubt troubled him.

Danser came stepping briskly towards him, notebook and pencil in his hand, an eager expression on his face.

'A rumour reached me – is it true Savage is inside with Milton?'

Archer ignored him. Eddie nodded, and Danser looked at the open door of the bank.

'Quiet enough. Maybe I can just—'

Archer said curtly. 'Nobody goes in till this is over. Back off.'

Danser shrugged and turned away; he crossed the street and joined the three women.

Then Butch, tagged by some of the roughs from the Last Round-up, came hurrying towards the bank.

'Is Savage still inside?'

'Keep out of this,' Archer told them. 'I'll not have a free-for-all – this is a private matter, to be settled privately.'

Butch grinned. 'Guess Milton will—'

The silence was shattered. Something – a table? – went over with a crash inside the bank. A voice – Christian's voice – screamed, 'Hurt him!'

Savage came to his feet, fingers clawed, teeth bared. He was hurting and someone had to be made to pay. He limped towards the door, needing space to weave and dodge. Milton, built like a gorilla, had an advantage at close quarters, and, with his leg dragging, Savage was too slow.

Milton looped a fist over and down, slamming him against the door. Savage twisted away as the big bodyguard tried to land another punch; the iron rings just grazed him with enough force to send him sliding to the floor. A heavy boot struck him and pain shot through his thigh.

Christian Howard brandished his sword from

153

his wheelchair. He crowed, 'That's it – make the Northern scum crawl!'

Savage got half-way upright when Milton hammered him with both fists and rocked him back on his heels. He sagged, gulping air. He grabbed a chair to use as a shield, but Milton tore it out of his hands and smashed it over his head.

Half stunned, he fell back as the bodyguard crowded him, kicking at his ribs. He shuddered, bruised and bleeding. Milton came at him, chopping his fists down with his weight behind them, driving him into a corner.

'Enough!' Christian snapped. 'You've got him now – but I want the whole town to see you finish him. The people of Rattle must be taught a lesson. I'm here to stay and I'm going to run things my way.'

Milton paused reluctantly.

'Throw him out,' Christian commanded. 'Cripple him in the street for everyone to see it doesn't pay to cross Christian Howard!'

Milton picked Savage up as easily as he would a baby and Savage let himself go slack so the bodyguard took his full weight. He was carried along the passage to the open door of the bank. Archer and Eddie stepped aside to allow Milton on to the boardwalk.

Then he threw Savage into the wide, dusty expanse of Broadway.

There was a sudden intake of breath from the watchers on the far side of the street as Savage hit the ground and rolled. A small cloud of dust erupted, and one of the townsmen groaned.

The stem of Naomi's pipe snapped in her hands, and she scowled.

'Damn! That was my best pipe too ...'

Danser laughed, and tension eased; at last something could be seen to be happening.

Archer raised his gun and called, 'Nobody interferes,' as Milton stepped down from the boardwalk.

Kate shouted back, 'That goes for you too!'

Rebecca watched closely, eyes shining in her dusky face. Men fighting was nothing new in her world, and she fancied herself a judge of quality.

'Two to one on Savage,' she offered the townsmen around her.

Kate looked startled, disapproving.

Michael Howard slowly shook his head.

'No, thanks. Milton's got the muscle and looks impressive, but Savage has a brain.'

Savage lay still, resting, taking in air and testing each limb in turn. He felt pain and a need to kill, but nothing seemed broken. He clenched his hands, waiting, and his expression might have made a mountain lion pause.

They'd made a serious mistake and his eyes glowed with pure cruelty; they'd given him room to manoeuvre and he aimed to kill first Milton and then Christian.

The sun was baking him and he squinted his eyes against the glare. He watched Christian roll his wheelchair out through the doorway of the bank and on to the boardwalk, waving his sword excitedly. That won't save you, Savage thought.

Archer and his deputy, Butch, and the hard-cases from the saloon moved back to give Christian room. Lew stood in the doorway of his shop ... and then Milton came striding towards him, ponderous and very sure of himself.

'Cripple him,' Christian shouted. 'Jump on him – pulp him!'

Savage edged away, looking for a weapon, anything to take care of Milton so he could get at the murderous cripple in the wheelchair.

Each movement brought fresh pain and tears of rage blurred his vision. He remembered the bullies on New York's waterfront; he'd beaten them and he'd beat this one.

From the corner of his eye he caught sight of movement close by; a long sinuous shape, silent, slowly winding its way through the dust, its ochre mottling making it almost invisible. Rattlesnake.

As Milton reached him, it raised its head to peer at the giant looming above; snakes were not used to being disturbed in this town. Milton raised a boot to stamp the Pinkerton into the ground.

Desperate, Savage grabbed the rattlesnake behind the head – he found the scales dry to his touch – and hurled it at Milton's face. Its curved teeth sank into flesh and it hung there, suspended from his cheek as the fangs injected their poison.

Milton screamed and stumbled around in panic. The snake dropped to the ground and glided away. Milton had two holes in his cheek and the flesh began to swell. He lost colour and held his face in his hands, sobbing and moaning. He staggered like a drunk. His bowed legs trembled and finally collapsed under him. He lay in the dust, twitching and crying.

Savage got to his feet with a chilling laugh. One down and one to go. He hobbled towards the boardwalk where Christian waited, sitting in his wheelchair and gripping a cavalry sword. Those close to him took one look at Savage's face and scattered.

The banker gave a wild shout.

'I'm here, Savage! Come and taste Southern steel. You won't find me so easy!'

Savage paused, studying the situation. Christian was alone now. He reached the boardwalk and stepped up.

He heard excited shouts from the crowd; nobody had ever challenged Mr Christian before. Savage glanced about him, looking for space to manoeuvre, an advantage. Then he backed towards Lew's shop.

Christian wheeled his chair along the planks, faster and faster, charging with a wild Rebel yell, a chairborne warrior with his sword extended before him. Savage dodged to one side and the blade missed him.

He stopped outside Lew's shop, waiting for Christian to turn his chair. Christian wheeled about, excited. Perhaps he had memories of the war when he rode men down and skewered them. His voice was hoarse.

'Charge!'

He trundled forward, gathering speed, sword slashing wildly.

Savage timed his approach and sprang high – the sword ripping his trouserleg and slicing flesh – to grab the striped barber's pole over the doorway and swing his legs up as Christian passed beneath.

Christian checked his rush and turned again, ready to return.

Savage swung on the pole, feeling it give under his weight; he kept swinging until it snapped. When he landed on the boardwalk he held a spear with a jagged point where the wood had splintered. He was ready to face Christian now, his teeth bared in a tiger's grin.

Christian Howard charged, sword extended before him.

'This time, Savage,' he yelled, 'you're a dead man!'

Savage didn't run or try to dodge. He waited, improvised spear held level.

Too late Christian realized that Savage wouldn't run and that the spear was longer than his blade. He was travelling too fast to stop and his furious charge impaled him on the jagged wooden point while his steel barely scratched Savage. The sword fell from his grasp and his eyes bulged.

'No...!'

Savage thrust hard and the spear went through him till it touched the chair, which came to a halt. Christian's face twisted at the shock and the light faded from his eyes. His head dropped forward.

Silence descended like a shroud.

Eddie stared in disbelief. Milton dead, now Mr Christian. Three women ran across the road but they were running to Savage; he felt weak with relief as he realized he didn't have to face them over the barrel of a gun.

Dr Jack pushed through the crowd to attend to the survivor.

But still, Savage had killed two men and the marshal. He looked around but couldn't see Archer anywhere.

Eddie stood still, considering, and began to sweat and shiver. Just the thought of going up against Savage, a man who'd survived impossible odds, gave him the shakes.

He saw Tom Archer coming from the livery, riding his horse. As Archer drew level, he unpinned his badge and tossed it to his deputy, then continued out of town.

Eddie caught the badge automatically and felt he was holding something red hot. Marshal? No thanks! The realization came that it took more than a gun to police a town.

Deputy, maybe, for now. If they still wanted him. His throat dry, he turned and hurried away.